The Silver Trumpet

Published by Barfield Press

Books by Owen Barfield:

The Silver Trumpet
Poetic Diction: A Study in Meaning
Romanticism Comes of Age
This Ever Diverse Pair
Saving the Appearances: A Study in Idolatry
Worlds Apart: A Dialogue of the 1960's
Unancestral Voice
Speaker's Meaning
What Coleridge Thought
The Rediscovery of Meaning, and Other Essays
History, Guilt and Habit
Owen Barfield on C. S. Lewis
Night Operation
Eager Spring
The Rose on the Ash-Heap
The Riddle of the Sphinx: Essays

Translations:

The Case for Anthroposophy

Forthcoming new editions:

Orpheus: A Poetic Drama
English People
Short Stories
Poetry
Plays

www.owenbarfield.org

Owen Barfield

The Silver Trumpet

Barfield Press
OXFORD, ENGLAND

Published by Barfield Press, Oxford, England, 2025
First published by Faber & Gwyer, London, 1925

Barfield Press edition of *The Silver Trumpet*
Text editor: Rory O'Connor
Illustrations: Fredy Jaramillo Serna
Cover: Gabriel Schenk

General Editor: Rory O'Connor

A catalogue record for this book is available from
the British Library.

The Silver Trumpet by Owen Barfield
ISBN 978-0-9569423-9-5 (hardcover)
ISBN 978-0-9569423-8-8 (paperback)
ISBN 978-1-917089-00-5 (ebook)

Printed on paper with Sustainable Forestry Initiative
(SFI) accreditation

Produced on behalf of
the Owen Barfield Literary Estate.

The Literary Estate promotes and safeguards the
works and intellectual legacy of Arthur Owen Barfield.

www.owenbarfield.org

CONTENTS

Foreword　　vii

Part I　　**1**

Chapter I　　1

Chapter II　　21

Chapter III　　29

Chapter IV　　45

Part II　　**55**

Chapter V　　55

Chapter VI　　67

Chapter VII　　77

Chapter VIII　　85

Chapter IX　　87

Chapter X　　95

Part III　　**107**

Chapter XI　　107

Chapter XII　　119

Chapter XIII　　135

Chapter XIV　　143

Chapter XV　　151

FOREWORD

The Silver Trumpet was written in 1924, and first published in 1925. It is the first children's fairy tale to have been published by one of those who came to be called the Inklings. They were a circle of writers who valued the imagination for its capacity to delight, as well as to summon up deep truths within us. They included C. S. Lewis, J. R. R. Tolkien and my grandfather, Owen Barfield.

Grandfather wrote *The Silver Trumpet* mostly because he wanted to write a good story. But, as he also later said, he had chosen "to bring out... the importance of the feeling element in life".

We see that importance again and again in the story. Early on, it is feeling that allows Prince Courtesy to discern the different natures of the twin princesses: his beloved, the good-natured Violet, and the "wicked" Gambetta. Kind feelings allow Violet to be open to the world, while harsh ones keep Gambetta cut off. And feelings of fear and courage stop or embolden many different adventures by princes and princesses later on in the tale.

The silver trumpet in this story brings the best feelings into everyone's hearts — and then everything in their world looks alive with possibility for a time. I hope that *The Silver Trumpet* will have the same effect on its readers.

Owen A. Barfield
Grandson
Oxfordshire, England

PART I

CHAPTER I

ONCE UPON A time there were two little Princesses whose names were Violetta and Gambetta; and they lived in Mountainy Castle. They were twins, and they were so like each other that when Violetta came in from a walk with her feet wet, Gambetta was sometimes told to go and change her stockings, because the Queen couldn't tell which from the other. But that didn't often happen, because if Princess Violetta was out for a walk, Princess Gambetta was almost sure to be out with her. Indeed they were so fond of one another that you might have thought they were tied together with a piece of string. All the same, the Queen used to be so fussed and worried by the confusion that, what with one thing and another, she persuaded the King to appoint a special Lord to distinguish between them. And he was called the Lord High Teller of the Other from Which. The first thing he did, after he was given this office, was to decree that everyone should call them by shorter names, because, as he said, their names both ended with "etta", and that made it much harder to tell.

"Why does it make it harder to tell?" said the King. "I don't see why it should make it harder."

"Never mind why, Your Majesty," the Lord High Teller replied firmly, "but it *does*."

"Very well," said His Majesty, "I think you are rather a fool, but I will do as you say, and I will see that my subjects do as you say, because this is your job and not mine." And he went off hunting.

So after that one of the sisters was called Princess Violet and the other was called Princess Gamboy.

Now, as it happened, the Lord High Teller of the Other from Which was not a fool at all but a very wise man. He had noticed something about the two little Princesses which nobody else had noticed. Moreover he knew a great deal about the magic power of names, for, soon after he had given them these new names, everybody else began to notice the same thing too. And before very long it was the rarest thing in the world for anybody about the Court to mistake one for the other. But first you must know how it came about that these two Princesses were so much alike, even after they were quite tall girls.

Well, the King and Queen had had a party at their christening, and among all the grand people they had asked Miss Thomson to step in. Now Miss Thomson was a relation by marriage of the Queen's and she was a nobody and she wasn't of the Blood Royal, or else she wouldn't have been called Miss Thomson. She lived in a little cottage in Tyttenhanger Lane. But the Queen had heard tell that this Miss Thomson was growing a witchery sort of woman in her old age, and that she knew this and that. So she said to the King: "If we don't ask her she may turn sour and come in at the

window of her own accord on a broomstick and do this and that. But, if we ask her to come, come she will because of the Christening Breakfast, and she may bring the babies a present worth all the golden rattles and silver teaspoons, and mahogany rocking-horses with real hair and eyes that move up and down in the world." So they sent her an invitation and she came. She was dressed in black and, when she walked, she leaned on a black stick with a silver handle, and of course her hat was narrower at the top than it was at the bottom. Her eyes were black, too, and didn't they sparkle! Now when she had finished her bacon and toast and marmalade she went up to the cradles, where all the grand people were standing about talking, and leaned over them. And the King and Queen, who had been watching her all the time from the other end of the room, held their breaths very hard and said, "Now it's coming, now it's coming," to themselves, as she leaned over the cradles.

Then the corners of Miss Thomson's mouth began to go into little creases, and she looked so whimsical and said very solemnly, waving her stick and looking at the King and Queen out of the corner of her eye:

Fumble, Fumble
    All around tumble,
Baby Princesses,
    Always be
As like as one
    To another pea;
This gifty I give
For as long as ye live,
Fumble, Fumble,
    All around tumble.

Then she went up to the King and Queen and said politely: "I am afraid I must be going now, Your Majesties; thank you so much!" The Queen said: "Not at all!" and she added, "Thank you very much for your kind present to my daughters."

"It was magic," said Miss Thomson.

"I know," said the Queen, who was really bitterly disappointed that Miss Thomson hadn't given her babies something nicer.

"It was magic you wanted," said Miss Thomson sharply.

"Yes," said the Queen humbly.

Now this Miss Thomson was really a kind-hearted old lady and she couldn't bear to see the Queen look so disappointed, especially after such a lovely breakfast. So she said, "Wait a minute," and went back to the cradles again. And this time there were no creases round her mouth, and she didn't wave her stick; but she frowned and looked hard into the little Princesses' eyes and said quietly:

"As long as you both live, you shall love each other more than all else in the world. As long as one of you is living, both shall *be*."

Then she went back to the King and Queen and said in a businesslike voice:

"Now I really *must* be going."

But the Queen, who had heard what she said over the cradles, fell suddenly on her knees and wept tears of joy, thanking dear Miss Thomson over and over again, kissing her hands and saying: "I don't deserve it, I don't deserve it. I only asked you here because I hoped you would give my daughters a present. I don't deserve it. Oh, now I know that my daughters will make each other happy."

"Don't be too sure about that!" said Miss Thomson, and bowed out of the room backwards, like the little lady she was.

That was how it came about that the two Princesses were so like each other, and that was how it came about that they were so fond of each other. Of course it would have been quite easy to tell them apart by making them dress in different clothes; but unfortunately there was a law in that country that all princesses were to wear the same clothes, until they reached the age of twenty-one, when they might choose for themselves. Indoors they had to wear little sky-blue tunics with silver-grey stockings, and out of doors a little black cloak over it all.

As for their hair, a princess in that country was banished at once if she was found with her hair plaited, or tied up with a bow, or anything of that sort. "𝔚𝔥𝔢𝔯𝔢𝔞𝔰 𝔰𝔥𝔢 𝔰𝔥𝔞𝔩𝔩 𝔥𝔞𝔳𝔢 𝔥𝔢𝔯 𝔥𝔞𝔦𝔯 𝔱𝔬 𝔥𝔞𝔫𝔤 𝔩𝔬𝔬𝔰𝔢𝔩𝔶 𝔡𝔬𝔴𝔫 𝔥𝔢𝔯 𝔟𝔞𝔠𝔨, 𝔞𝔫𝔡 𝔴𝔢𝔩𝔩 𝔨𝔢𝔢𝔪𝔢𝔡." That was what the law said, meaning "well combed". It was only in the Royal Nursery or in the West Corner of the Queen's Garden that Violetta and Gambetta were allowed to wear just what they liked and to do their hair just as they pleased.

What was it that the Lord High Teller of the Other from Which had noticed about the two Princesses, before he had their names altered? One day he was walking in the garden to take the air, when he saw the two sisters playing together near the entrance-gate. Just then a little ragged boy passed along the road outside, crying and crying. Violetta's eyes filled with

tears, and she ran out and gave him an apple she had in her hand and asked him what was the matter. The Lord High Teller couldn't hear what she said or what the little boy said, but he saw the little boy gradually stop crying as he listened, and go off at last with his face all shining. Then the Princess Violetta came back to her sister, and the Lord High Teller heard them talking to each other.

"What are you crying about?" said Gambetta.

"I can't help it," said Violetta, "I am thinking of all the other little ragged boys. Oh dear, I am so miserable." And she went on crying.

"Don't be silly," said Gambetta, "I expect he started crying like that on purpose to make you give him your apple."

"Why should you think so?" said Violetta.

"People are like that," said Gambetta.

"I don't believe it," said Violetta through her tears.

"You'll learn in time, my dear," said Gambetta, who was one minute older than her sister.

The Noble Lord didn't hear any more of their conversation, but he smiled rather sadly to himself as he walked on. And a week later, when the King appointed him Lord High Teller of the Other from Which, he knew quite well, of course, that the Princesses ought to be called Violet and Gamboy. And they were.

From that time on the King and Queen and the whole Court gradually began to see what the Lord High Teller had seen already. It was this: The two little Princesses, who were so much alike on the outside that you couldn't tell them apart, were as different

inside as a Church from a Booking Office. But the two spells which Miss Thomson had laid on them at their christening remained unbroken. When Princess Gamboy had said so many sour things that an ugly wrinkle began to show in her face, the same wrinkle began to show in Princess Violet's face, whether she liked it or not. But, on the other hand, when Princess Violet had danced and sung so much (for she was very fond of singing and dancing) and made so many people happy that two quite new dimples appeared on both sides of her mouth, the same dimples appeared on both sides of Princess Gamboy's mouth, whether she liked it or not. Of course the dimples and wrinkles got in each other's way a good deal, and the dimples were not quite so pretty and the wrinkles not quite so ugly as they might have been. In short, while Princess Gamboy was not *nearly* so ugly as she would otherwise have been, neither was Princess Violet *quite* so beautiful. That was what the spell did. As for the other spell, the only thing in the whole world which Princess Gamboy loved was Princess Violet, and, among the hundreds of thousands of things which Princess Violet loved, Princess Gamboy, no matter what she might say or do, was far and away the first. They could not bear to be out of each other's company for an hour, although, when they were together, they did nothing but argue and have conversations like the one which the Lord High Teller overheard.

So the two Princesses grew up side by side in the Castle until one morning when Princess Violet was dancing, as a leaf dances in the wind, in the West Corner of the Queen's Garden, and Princess Gamboy

was reading in a big black book called *Excerpta* and continually looking up and saying to Violet, "Keep still, can't you!" they heard a silver trumpet sounding faintly in the distance. Princess Violet knew it must be a silver one, because the noise it made was like a bell. But Princess Gamboy said rudely:

"Nonsense. I don't believe you can tell what it's made of. And if it is, it's ridiculous to waste so much of the public money on a trumpet. Silver indeed! Tut!"

And she bent her head down over her book again, frowning and mumbling something which sounded to Violet like "Formforze ate Toosten." Poor Violet felt crushed, but she didn't say anything, and ran straight off to the gate to see who it was; for she felt quite sure the trumpet had been blown by someone on his way to the Castle. She pressed her forehead against the bars of the gate and made two white marks on it; but there was nothing to be seen yet in the dusty white road leading away up over the hills. Then, suddenly, she heard the trumpet again, and this time it sounded a little nearer:

Rooty ^{tootity} ^{tootity} ^{tootity} ^{tootity} $^{too.}$ ^{Too} tootity tootity tootity $_{too.}$

Rooty $^{too.}$ Rooty $^{too.}$ Rooty $^{too-oo-oo.}$

"It *is* like a bell," she said to herself; "and I know it's made of silver." And she began to feel so happy because it seemed as though there must be a piece of silver somewhere inside her which was still vibrating on and on to the trumpet, till she fell in a dream in

which she was listening to church bells across the water on a summer evening. But then, right on top of the hill, where the road vanished into the sky, she saw a little cloud of dust. The cloud grew bigger, and she knew it was made by advancing horsemen. Then the trumpet-call again, ringing out clear and loud and joyous this time, as the sweet waves of sound welled from its mouth and spread out through the air until they lapped smoothly on her ear, unbroken by any wind.

Rooty ^{tootity} ^{tootity} ^{tootity} ^{tootity} $^{too.}$ Too $_{tootity}$ $_{tootity}$ $_{tootity}$ $_{too.}$

Rooty $^{too.}$ Rooty $^{too.}$ Rooty $^{too-oo-oo.}$

At last the dust began to clear a little, and Princess Violet could distinguish the figure of a tall young man on a white horse at the head of the party. He was clad in glittering silver armour — not that kind which is made in separate stiff pieces and makes a man look like five tin sausages, but the kind which is called "chain-mail". It is all woven in shining links, so that it looks like a million watch-chains and fits as close as wool.

Violet rushed back to where Gamboy was sitting.

"It's a *Prince*," she shrieked, and she waltzed around Gamboy singing over and over again a little song which meant absolutely nothing at all. It sounded like,

> "Create a sensation of glory
> All in the land of Judea."

She always sang it when she felt excited.

You see, they hardly ever had a visitor at Mountainy Castle, and Violet, happy as she was, sometimes felt dull and cross and tired of singing and dancing all by herself. But all Princess Gamboy said was:

"Well, don't get so excited about him; it will only make him more conceited than he is already."

"How do you know he is conceited already?" said Princess Violet.

"I don't know," answered Gamboy, "but they nearly always are."

"But you've never met any," said Princess Violet, "so how do you know?"

"Ah!" said Princess Gamboy, who was one minute older than her sister, and she smiled and wouldn't say any more.

Meanwhile the party of horsemen, with the Prince at its head, had reached the gate. Violet watched from behind a bush, where she could not be seen. She saw the Prince send forward a herald, who struck thrice on the bell with his riding-crop (for, although the Prince was in chain-mail, none of the party carried swords). Then the Prince himself moved his horse forward a few paces and told it to stand still. But the horse, instead of standing still, kept moving its feet about in a mincing little dance, as horses do. So, without waiting, the Prince stood up in his stirrups and taking a shining silver trumpet from his baldric.... ("There, it *is* silver," thought Violet, and she nearly went and told Gamboy, but she was too interested).... taking a shining silver trumpet from his baldric, he placed it to his lips and calmly blew:

Rooty ^{tootity} tootity tootity tootity ^{too.} Too tootity tootity tootity too.

Rooty ^{too.} Rooty ^{too.} Rooty ^{too-oo-oo.}

Now at the very first note of the trumpet, the Prince's horse, which had been criss-crossing its feet all this time, and shaking its head and behaving dainty, suddenly stiffened, pricked up both its ears, and stood as stock still as a marble horse. And at the very first note of the trumpet, Princess Violet forgot the Prince and the garden and Princess Gamboy and Mountainy Castle and the sky above her and dreamed she was afloat beneath tons and tons of clear green water near the bottom of the sea, and — oh, yes — far away someone was booming a huge bell. She couldn't hear it, but she could tell because all that great water shook. And at the very first note of the trumpet Princess Gamboy lost her place in the book where she was reading how "Formforze ate Toosten", and instead of being angry and shutting it with a bang, as she usually did when she lost the place, she leaned back in her garden-chair and began to think of the time when she was a little baby, before she was called Gamboy and before Violet and she grew so different from one another; and she even wondered for a moment whether she was really so very much wiser than her sister, even though she *was* a whole minute older. And at the very first note of the trumpet, all the porters and doorkeepers and sweepers and cooks and bakers and pastry-makers in Mountainy Castle stopped carrying and doorkeeping and sweeping and cooking and baking and pastry-making, and looked at each other and listened. And the head-porter didn't tell the under-porters to get on with their work, and the head-doorkeeper didn't tell the under-doorkeeper to get on with *his* work, and the head-sweeper and cook and baker and pastry-maker didn't tell the under-sweepers, cooks, bakers, and pastry-makers to get on with *their* work; but they all stood still, staring and listening like so many loons.

Rooty tootity tootity tootity tootity too. Too tootity tootity tootity too.

Rooty too. Rooty too. Rooty too-oo-oo.

As the last note died slowly away, everybody in the Castle stirred slowly, like a man waking from sleep, and looked mazedly round him; all were full of wonder, and many opened their mouths to ask their neighbours what had happened. But, just as they were about to speak, they seemed to change their minds; they turned their eyes away from each other and down to the ground, as though they were ashamed of something — as though they all knew something they were all pretending they didn't know — and went on with their work. Only the head-doorkeeper spoke. He told the under-doorkeeper to go and open the gate. And as the last note died slowly away, Princess Gamboy stirred and shook herself and opened her book again. "Don't be a fool, Gamboy," she said to herself (for she had a way of talking to herself). "*You* are a nice sensible girl. V. is a great silly. Ugh!" And as the last

note died slowly away, it seemed to Princess Violet that she was rising slowly through the silent green waters, which still shook all through to the booming of that unseen bell, until at last her head burst up into the open air, and, lo and behold! there was no water at all, and she was back in the Castle gardens looking at the Silver Prince, who had just taken the trumpet from his lips.

CHAPTER II

THE GATE WAS unbarred, and the Prince dismounted gravely from his horse and gave it to the herald to hold.

"Is His Majesty at home?" he inquired of the under-doorkeeper.

"His Majesty is at home, Sire, but he is about going a-hunting, and loves not to be delayed."

"Never mind," said the Prince boldly, "I demand an audience."

"By what right?" said the fellow sullenly.

"By my own right," sternly answered the Prince. "By the right of courtesy." And he handed the under-doorkeeper a polished mahogany tablet with

PRINCE COURTESY

engraved on it. "Take this to your master," he said, and turned away.

The under-doorkeeper louted low and went into the Castle. In a few moments the head-doorkeeper appeared and said with a low reverence:

"His Majesty awaits you, Sire, in the guest-chamber." Prince Courtesy followed the head-doorkeeper into the Castle, across the courtyard, and up a flight of fine stone steps to the guest-chamber, where the King was waiting.

"Your Majesty," said the Prince, "is doubtless aware that I am heir to the throne of the neighbouring kingdom of Dravidia. The King, my Father, has sent me abroad to seek adventures and to choose a maiden to be my Queen."

"Well," said the King, "it all depends what you mean by adventures. We have no dragons at Mountainy Castle, nor riddles to be solved, nor ogres to be slain, and the nearest thing we have to a witch is old Miss Thomson, who, though she is not of the Blood Royal, is a kindly old body and would not willingly harm a mouse. Besides, she doesn't live in the Castle. As to the second part of your request — I have two daughters. Need I say more?"

"Have I your consent then, Sire, to the hand of one of them?"

"You may have the hand of either of them, provided that you first win her heart, but that," said the King, rising from his chair, "is your job and not mine." And he went off hunting.

Prince Courtesy was rather dumbfounded at being left alone in a strange Castle. He did not know where to go, so he decided to stay where he was (until something happened), and sitting down patiently on a chair he began to ponder deeply how he could best follow his Father's instructions.

"Hullo, you!" said a voice.

Prince Courtesy looked up astonished, but saw no one.

"Hullo, you," said the voice again. "Who are you?"

This time the Prince saw who had spoken. Deep in the very biggest and reddest arm-chair in the room

was sitting a stout little Dwarf all dressed in red, so that you could hardly see him.

"I have been watching you think for ten minutes," said the Dwarf. "Does it hurt, and who are you?"

"I am Prince Courtesy," answered the Prince politely. "And may I perhaps inquire *your* name?"

"Oh, *me!*" said the Dwarf — and he climbed down off the chair, planted his minikin legs apart, and stuck out both his arms in one long, tremendous yawn — "*I* am the Little Fat Podger."

"I see," said the Prince, who was very much surprised indeed, "and will it be inquisitive to ask what you do?"

"Not in the least," answered the Little Fat Podger; "I am Curator of the Royal Dump."

"You are — ?" said the Prince.

"I cure the King's megrims, you know."

"Oh!" said Courtesy.

"Wit, you know — wit," said the Dwarf, "jokes, practical jokes, chestnuts, japes, jests, gibes, pranks, cheek, balder-dash, noodledum, nincompoopery, somersaults, tumbling, twinkling, capers, and the sidestep step, and the sidestep step, and the sidestep, sidestep, sidestep step."

As he said the last words he danced solemnly up and down the room keeping time to them and flopping his arms and legs about all loosely. He looked so absurd that the Prince leaned back in his chair and shouted with laughter. But the Little Fat Podger himself never even smiled. He stopped at last quite out of breath and looked across at the Prince.

"The Grotesque, you know — anything Gothic," he said gently.

Now the Prince was so polite that, as soon as he saw that the Dwarf wasn't joining in the laughter, he stopped, although it very much hurt his sides. And then the Dwarf came up to him and shook hands with him as though they had only just met.

"Can I be of any use to you?" he said. "Advice good and better, criticism of life, information about the Castle, introduction to the daughters of the house, etc., etc."

It was very curious. The Dwarf spoke so fast and used such funny long words that the Prince understood a good deal less than half of what he said. And yet he somehow *felt in his bones* that this queer little creature was good and meant kindly by him. HE FELT IT IN HIS BONES.

"Advice," he said thoughtfully, "yes, tell me where to find adventures. My father sent me out to seek adventures and choose a Queen, and I do feel the adventures ought to come first."

The Dwarf suddenly stood very still with his head perked on one side, like a startled sparrow.

"Did I understand you to say you were *looking* for adventures?" he said slowly.

"Yes."

"*Looking* for them?"

"Yes, looking for them," said the Prince.

"*Looking* for them?" said the Dwarf again, waggling his head.

The Prince began to get rather angry with this rude little man.

"You offered me your advice," he said. "I asked you a question, and all you do is to pretend you are deaf. It is unkind."

The Little Fat Podger bowed: "Apologies," he said, "amends, repentance, genuflexion, the *amende honorable* — anything refined. But — *looking* for them! Poor fellow, poor fellow." He came close up to the Prince, whisked on to the arm of his chair, and standing on tiptoe, whispered in his ear:

"Take my advice and don't make yourself absolutely *hot* over it!"

"Very well, then, can you take me to the Princesses?" said Courtesy.

"Follow me," said the Little Fat Podger, "to the West Corner of the Queen's Garden." And off they went.

CHAPTER III

WHEN THEY REACHED the Queen's Garden, the Dwarf pointed to a tall, dark yew-hedge, which looked very quiet and sleepy in the sunlight.

"You see that hedge?" he cried.

"Yes," said the Prince.

"Well," said the Dwarf, "the ladies are walking behind there. Good-bye!" And he suddenly gave a hop and a skip and a hop and a jump away from the Prince, murmuring busily to himself as he did so. "*One, two, three*, and *ON to it*."

"Hi!" shouted the Prince.

At this the Little Fat Podger, poised on one leg, looked back over his shoulder and sang a song:

> "Princesses, Princesses,
> Identical dresses,
>   And faces as like as peas — "

and he would have been off again, had not the Prince cried out appealingly that he might at least have told him the ladies' names. At that he twirled right round on his toe, and, after a pause, gave a leap back in the Prince's direction, saying as he landed on both feet,

> "Take Violetta."

Then he stood quite still and nodded twice very wisely, saying as he nodded,

"Much better, much better."

Then he took another leap towards the Prince, balanced on one foot, and shouted out quite loud,

"If you can get her."

Then he took *another* leap, landed right beside the Prince, stretched up on tiptoe, beckoned to him to bend his head down, and, seizing the Prince's hair in both hands, put his lips to his ear and whispered sharply,

"Without Gambetta."

At which the Little Fat Podger let go the Prince's head and danced oddly away, murmuring to himself, "*To the side, to the side, point, point, point. To the side, to the side, point, point, point,*" and so vanished into the Castle.

The poor Prince was very much bewildered by all this, and he did feel shy as he tiptoed across the wide green lawn which lay between him and the hedge. But when he went round the hedge, he found to his surprise that there was only one Princess there. She was sitting reading.

"This must be Violetta," he thought, for she looked very beautiful. So he went up to her, and kneeling on one knee, said humbly:

"Most Gracious Lady, pardon the intrusion of one who is as yet a stranger to you. If I am something too forward in my address, you must believe that it is your beauty which has stolen my manners."

But Princess Gamboy (for it was she) looked up from her book and said:

"Stuff!"

The poor Prince was so taken aback that he hadn't a word to say. He didn't know whether to get up or stay on his knees. At last, as he was not very clever, he said the same thing over again:

"Most Gracious Lady, pardon the intrusion of one who is as yet a stranger to you. If I am something too forward in my address, you must believe that it is your beauty which has stolen my manners."

Princess Gamboy went on reading.

" — M — which has — er — stolen my manners," repeated the Prince nervously. "Will you not vouchsafe — "

Princess Gamboy looked up and interrupted him:

"If my beauty has stolen your manners, young man, I should have thought the less said about it the better." And she got up, slammed her book, tucked it under her arm, and walked off.

In a little while Princess Violet came round the hedge to look for her sister. But the Prince, who thought it was Princess Gamboy come back again, pretended not to see her. She recognized him at once as the Silver Prince who had ridden up to the gate on horseback. So she sat down on Gamboy's chair and waited for him to speak. But as he continued to stand still with his face turned away from her, at last she rose and went to him, saying kindly:

"Most Gracious Prince, I fear you are weary after your long journey. Will you not come into the Castle and there rest yourself, after you have eaten and drunk your fill?"

"Ah, Lady," said Prince Courtesy sorrowfully, "that is kind of you: but how can I tell that even as you have just now changed from ungentle to kind, you will not change back again from kind to ungentle? Nay, I had rather be left alone." And he shook his head sorrowfully.

How politely they both talked to one another, using much longer words than they did at any other time! Wasn't it funny?

"I do not understand you, Prince," said Violet, "*I* change? How changed, when until now you have never seen me?"

"Five minutes ago — " began the Prince.

"I was with my Mother in the Castle," she said. But then the Prince suddenly remembered how the Dwarf had sung,

> "Princesses, Princesses,
> Identical dresses,
>   And faces as like as peas — "

Yes, faces, he thought to himself, *faces* as like as peas, oh, faces to be sure — but most certainly nothing else.

"I am sorry," he said humbly, "I thought you were Princess Gamboy." And he knelt and kissed Princess Violet's hand and rose and went with her into the Castle.

From that moment began one of the strangest
stories that could possibly be imagined. The Prince
stayed on at Mountainy Castle, and, of course, he and
Princess Violet grew quickly fonder of one another. It
was only at first that he actually used to mistake
Violet for Gamboy and Gamboy for Violet. That was
only at first, because very soon he knew quite well
which was which, without having to send a page for
the Lord High Teller. Nobody else could ever be quite
sure, but Prince Courtesy became so fond of Violet that
HE KNEW. But although, whenever he saw Gamboy, he
knew she *was* Gamboy, that didn't make any
difference to the fact that he saw very much too much
of her. It was the one thing about which he and Violet
could not agree. For while Violet still loved her sister
more than anything else in the world, more even than
Prince Courtesy himself, the Prince — well, he just
didn't love her at all. She was so hopelessly in the way.
It would take much too long to tell how she never left
them alone; how, when Violet was dancing to the
Prince in the West Corner of the Queen's Garden, she
would make sarcastic remarks in a loud voice about
people who wasted their time *jumping about like
toads*; how, when the Prince thanked Violet for
dancing so beautifully and made pretty speeches
about her little feet, Gamboy would get up from her
chair, slam her book, and say, "Little feet, indeed.
Tut!" — how, in fact, she always managed somehow
to spoil their happiness together. But one fine day the
Prince, who had brought some musicians along with
him in his train, ordered them after supper to come out
into the West Corner of the Queen's Garden.

First of all out came a man carrying a little fiddle, then came another man with another little fiddle, then came another man with a fiddle a little bigger than these, then another man with a fiddle nearly as big as himself, but lastly a fifth man came with a fiddle so simply enormous that he could hardly carry it. And the men were all dressed in pink, with white frills round their wrists and necks, and yellow stockings, and curly grey wigs on their heads. They sat down and scraped their fiddles once or twice with their fiddling-sticks. Meanwhile Gamboy was grumbling surlily at not being left to read in peace, because of the deafening noise they were making. Prince Courtesy would have liked to say, "Well, go away then!" but he knew Violet wouldn't like it, so he kept silence. But at last the musicians stopped scraping.

There they all sat still, in the yellow sunlight, with the dark yew-hedge behind them.

Then the first man began to play a little tune on his little fiddle, and before he had got very far the second man began to play the same tune on *his* little fiddle, but the first man didn't stop playing his little tune — oh no, he went straight on; and then the third man began to play the same tune on *his* fiddle, and the fourth man on his, and lastly the fifth man began that very same tune on his great big fiddle, so low down that it sounded like growling thunder.

Now Violet and Gamboy had never heard anything like this before, and, as the music played on, they dreamed that the sounds coming from the five fiddles were five shining silk threads, each of a different colour, twisting and twining and curling and winding

in and out and over and under one another in a
marvellous pattern and always moving on and on and
on, till Violet thought, "It's better than dancing," and
Gamboy thought — well, as a matter of fact she
thought of nothing at all. Which was a very unusual
thing for her to do. But the curious thing was that
when the music stopped, Princess Gamboy sat on in
silence with her hands folded across her lap, staring
away into nothing. And all the rest of that evening she
never spoke one harsh word. Later on the three of
them wandered round the Queen's Garden, just as the
sun was setting and a great golden moon rising out of
the mist opposite. And the Prince put his arm through
Violet's and Violet put her arm through Gamboy's and
they were all three of them so quiet and happy that
they never forgot that evening all the rest of their
lives. Sometimes, when they were very miserable and
hot and tired, the memory of it would suddenly come
back to them like a cool breeze blowing on their
foreheads and make them happy again.

The next morning the Prince, who had grown very
friendly with the Little Fat Podger, told him about this
and asked him what he thought it might mean.

"Music hath charms," said the Dwarf. "Harmony,
you know, harmony — Form versus Chaos — Light v.
Darkness — and the Dominant Seventh. It's all one."

The Prince thought this was rather foolish. It was
advice he wanted, and he now asked the Dwarf point
blank how he might keep Gamboy for ever in her
gentle mood.

"Prince," said the Dwarf, planting his legs very wide
apart, "you are a nin-a-kin." And he opened his legs

wider and wider (for he had very few bones), and slid down till they stuck out flat on the floor each side of him. Then he jumped up and slapped both his thighs one after the other very quickly, saying:

"*One, two!*"

"What about the Silver Trumpet?" he shouted, and he slapped both the Prince's knees, "*One, Two!*" so that the poor Prince howled with surprise. But before he recovered himself, the Little Fat Podger was gone.

What does he mean? thought Courtesy. Then he remembered the Silver Trumpet hanging from his baldric, the one he had blown so boldly at the Castle gate.

That afternoon Gamboy was at her old tricks again. But just as she was beginning to say something nasty and sneery about Princes, Prince Courtesy took the Silver Trumpet from his baldric and blew.

"Your Princes," Gamboy was saying, speaking half through her nose, "are — "

(Prince Courtesy reached out his hand towards the trumpet.)

" — very fine *gentlemen*, no doubt — "

(Prince Courtesy's fingers closed on the handle.)

" — but whether that's a — "

(The trumpet was at Prince Courtesy's lips.)

"*compliment —*

Rooty tootity tootity tootity tootity too.

Princess Gamboy gulped back the rest of the words and turned her nose down.

Too
      tootity tootity tootity tootity too.

Princess Gamboy's mouth shut with a snap,

Rooty ^{too.} Rooty ^{too.} Rooty ^{too-oo-oo.}

Princess Gamboy folded her hands in her lap and leaned back in the chair, staring far and far away into nothingness. She was dreaming. And oh — she was silent!

After that Violet and the Prince were much happier, for the Prince had only to blow his trumpet to bring them peace and the quiet they loved. Nevertheless their troubles were by no means at an end, nor was Gamboy subdued. As soon as the drowsy dream brought upon her by the Silver Trumpet began to fade, she would open her mouth and start carping and sneering more than ever. So that the Prince would have to put the trumpet to his lips and blow again; and it was a tiresome thing to be continually making this odd noise all over the Castle grounds. Moreover, if by any chance he left the trumpet behind in his room one day, or if the mouth-piece was clogged up so that it wouldn't blow, they were at the mercy of Gamboy's horrid tongue. At such times she seemed to be bitterer than ever, not because she had anything to complain of, but as though she were making up for all the time she had lost beneath the spell of the Silver Trumpet. Thus, although Violet and the Prince could be sure of any number of peaceful half-hours together, yet in a way matters grew worse and worse, for Gamboy had

become so sharp and ill-natured that she and the Prince frequently quarreled openly. After these quarrels the Prince would always feel very worried and miserable; "She is Violet's beloved sister," he would say to himself, thinking sadly of the loud, unkind voice in which he had reproved her and the many things he wished he had not said, because they had hurt poor Violet's tender heart.

At last the Prince asked Violet if she would marry him and be his Queen.

She told him to wait until the following day, when she would give him her answer. Now she was certain in her own mind that the answer would be "Yes"; but all the same she wanted to tell somebody and pretend to ask their advice. So she set out to look for Gamboy, who had been left indoors. But on the way she met the Dwarf, and he was such a very great friend of hers that she decided to tell *him*.

So she told him.

"Hooray!" shouted the Little Fat Podger. "The answer is in the affirmative," and he seized hold of Princess Violet's knees, for he couldn't reach any higher, and insisted on teaching her there and then a new dance, shrieking excitedly, *"To the right, step, step. To the left, step, step. Behind, to the side, in front, hop."*

They danced up and down together.

"Now I am going to tell Gamboy," said Violet breathlessly.

"What's that?" said the Dwarf, stopping short.

"I am going to tell Gamboy," said Violet.

"Don't!" said the Dwarf.

"Shall!" said Violet, still laughing.

"Don't!" said the Dwarf.

"Shall," said the Princess, jumping up and down.

Now the Little Fat Podger hated Gamboy as much as he loved Violet, and it was a source of great sorrow to him that Violet could be so fond of anybody so disagreeable. He longed to separate them. Suddenly he changed his mind.

"Yes, do!" he said, "and, when you have told her, listen very carefully to what she says."

That Dwarf was a wise little fellow. He knew a hawk from a handsaw, and, what is more, he knew Princess Gamboy's heart inside out.

So Violet went dancing off into the Castle;

> "Create a sensation of glory
> All in the land of Judea,"

she sang, till she came to where Princess Gamboy was. She was sitting in a high-backed chair, casting up the accounts of the *Amalgamated Princesses' Society*.

"Gamboy, dear," she began shyly — "Gamboy, darling — I say, 'Betta!" And she went on and told her everything. But, when she had finished, Princess Gamboy behaved in the most unexpected way; for she got up from her chair, tucked her book under one arm, and with her hands clasped behind her back began to stride up and down the room in silence, frowning angrily. At last she stopped and turned sharply to Violet.

"Listen, Violet," she said, "I hate that Prince, and if you marry him, I'll have no more to do with you."

But, 'Betta!" said Violet, opening her eyes wide with astonishment, "*why* do you hate him?"

"Because," answered Gamboy, "because — what's that to you, Miss? I hate him. Now — which of us are you going to choose?"

Violet began to cry, "Oh, 'Betta, 'Betta," she said, "why won't you understand? He loves me. And — and — I love him."

"Understand!" snapped Gamboy. "Stuff! Don't you imagine that *love* butters any parsnips. He *said* he loved you. Oh yes, he *said* he loved you. Of course he did — they all say that. Do you know what he really loves? Himself. You admire him so much that when he looks into your silly great eyes he thinks himself the finest fellow that ever was. That's what he loves. They may say what they like of little Gamboy, but she's no fool. Oh no, my dears, she's no fool!"

Princess Gamboy was so much pleased with her little speech that she began to strut triumphantly up and down the room, repeating the last words to herself under her breath. But inside Princess Violet's head something seemed to snap suddenly, as though an elastic band had been broken there. It was the spell cast on her by old Miss Thomson at the christening, for there was one thing in the world strong enough to break it, and that was her love for Prince Courtesy. But she did not know this, for she had never heard of the spell. She only knew that something very strange had happened to her, and from that moment on she loved Prince Courtesy more than she loved anything else in the world. But she still loved Princess Gamboy next best. She stopped crying, and without saying a word looked straight into her sister's eyes. Gamboy stopped still, and the two Princesses stood for a whole minute looking at each other in silence. But then Princess Gamboy's eyes fell to the ground abashed, and Princess Violet turned and left the room. She found the Prince waiting in the garden.

"Courtesy," she cried; "you needn't wait till tomorrow. The answer is 'Yes!'"

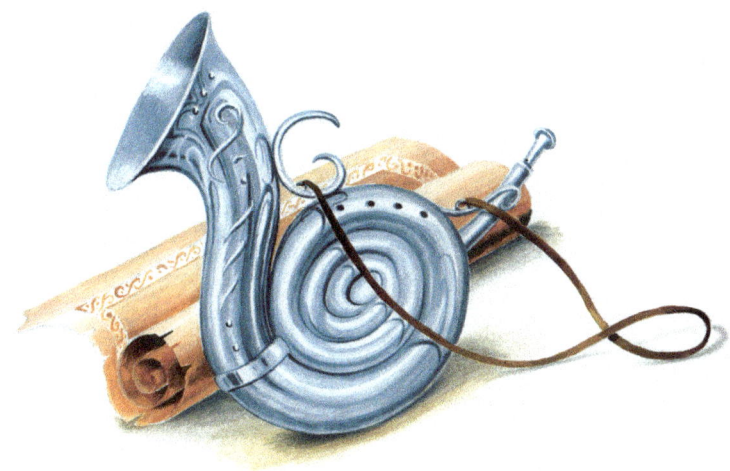

CHAPTER IV

AND NOW THE story must hurry on, for there are many more things to be told yet, so many, that if you knew all that is still to happen you would say it had scarcely begun. Therefore you must try and imagine to yourself what took place in the next few months; how happy the Prince and Violet were together in spite of Gamboy's ill-nature; how for a long time she refused to speak to either of them, and how unhappy this made Violet, though the Prince didn't care a rap. But although she wouldn't speak to them, neither would she leave them alone. You see, it would have been very little pleasure to her to sulk alone in her room and from her window see them walking and whispering together down in the garden. So she contrived to be always waiting round the corner, and as soon as they came near, she would get up from her chair, pull her skirts about her, and march away with her head in the air without looking at them. Or if they came into a room in the Castle, she was sure to be sitting there already, and she would get up and go out, slamming the door after her. This always made poor Violet feel unhappy for quite a long time, and even the Prince would feel uncomfortable, which was just what Princess Gamboy wanted. You may be surprised that she should still have wanted Violet to feel unhappy, when she loved her better than anything else in the world; but there are two ways of loving people: one is to like seeing them well and happy, which was Violet's way of loving, and the other is to like them to do what you tell them to, which was Gamboy's way.

One day Princess Violet stopped Princess Gamboy and asked her why she was so angry with her, and Gamboy raised her eyebrows and answered coldly:

"My dear child, I am not in the least angry with you. Why should I be angry? I am only concerned for your own happiness. I am sure I hope you will *always* be as happy as you are *now*." And she swept out of the room and left Violet crying. But the Prince frowned and said:

"Stuff!"

Which was quite right, because it was all lies from beginning to end, and he knew it.

And you must also imagine to yourself how the preparations went forward for the wedding, and how the Prince began to feel horribly nervous lest, in the excitement of the moment, he should find himself *married to Gamboy instead of Violet.* How dreadful that would have been! But remember that the two Princesses, in accordance with the law, were dressed exactly alike, and both wore their hair hanging loosely down their backs *and* well keemed. It might happen, you know. So at last in his perplexity the Prince went for advice to the Little Fat Podger. And when he had told him his trouble, the Little Fat Podger stood thinking for a while and then skipped away with three great grasshoppery, jiggery jumps, looking back over his shoulder and crying out at each step,

"Twiddlem
Twaddlem
Twenty-one."

How puzzled the poor Prince was, till suddenly he remembered having been told that the law about the Princesses only held good till their twenty-first birthday, and then he understood what the Dwarf meant. So he delayed the preparations for the wedding, in spite of his impatience, and arranged that they should be married on Violet's twenty-first birthday, when she would be able to wear what she pleased.

At last, at last, the longed-for morning came, and at breakfast-time everybody waited to see what kind of clothes the two Princesses would wear. Of course they had both looked forward very much to the day when they would be able to wear what they pleased, and each of them, without saying a word to the other, had been secretly preparing her new dress for a month past. Yes, even Gamboy was pleased and excited about this, for, as she said, it was not the clothes themselves that mattered, but *the liberty to choose them for yourself.* By which she meant the liberty to make yourself look as ugly as you pleased.

Gamboy came down first, and everybody gasped to see how different she looked from yesterday. She had put on a narrow, straight, skimpy black dress, which was no wider at the bottom than it was at the top, so that she looked like an umbrella-stand; as for her hair, she had just taken hold of it with both hands, pulled it back as far as it would go over the top of her head, and tied it there with three pieces of string. But she had tied it so tightly that her eyes looked as though they were starting from her head with surprise. She did look funny. And when they saw Gamboy's hair, all the ladies-in-waiting at the breakfast-table put down their knives and forks and let their bacon get cold, while they giggled and tittered to each other:

"She's done it in a bun, she's done it in a bun!"

"What's that?" said Gamboy sharply. And everybody dropped their eyes and picked up their knives and forks and went on eating in silence. But then the door opened and Princess Violet came in! She was dressed in white from head to foot and her skirt fell spreading from her waist so lightly that she seemed to float on air. And her beautiful long hair was piled and piled on top of her head up against a marvellous comb, made of old silver, which rose above it at the back like a tower on the top of a rocky hill, or like St. Michael's Mount in Cornwall. And once again everybody put down their knives and forks and stared. They stared at her in amazement, for yesterday she had been a pretty little girl and now it seemed she was a beautiful lady. How glad Prince Courtesy was that he had waited till her twenty-first birthday! And even the King, who had come downstairs in a bad temper, because he was to go to the wedding that day instead of going hunting, even the King smiled with delight, and rose and kissed his daughter and was most sweet-tempered all the rest of the day. "No fear of mistaking them *now*," thought Courtesy to himself, and indeed it would be hard to imagine two more different people. Their very faces no longer looked the same, though of course they were exactly the same really; and if Princess Gamboy had cared, she could have made herself look as beautiful as her sister.

When Violet and Gamboy had opened all their parcels (for people receive more presents on their

twenty-first birthday than on any other), there was a tremendous bustle throughout the Castle, and everybody, from the Lord High Teller of the Other from Which (who no longer had any work to do, but still went on drawing a high salary for it from the King's Treasury) to the smallest and dirtiest of the stable boys, began to scrub himself up and put on his best clothes in readiness to start for the Church. At eleven o'clock every soul in the Castle started off in a long winding procession, some in chariots, some on horseback, some in sedan chairs, and some afoot, to go to the Church, which lay a mile off.

The wedding, too, you must imagine for yourself, and how Princess Gamboy, in her skimpy black dress, sat in the front row and glowered at the bride and bridegroom all the while it was going on. She would have frowned as well, only she had tied her hair back so tightly that she couldn't move her forehead. But as the party came out of the Church, the Prince's herald, who had been stationed at the door, put the Silver Trumpet to his lips and blew. And the sound that came out of the mouth of the trumpet was

Rooty ^{tootity} ^{tootity} ^{tootity} ^{tootity} $^{too.}$ Too $_{tootity}$ $_{tootity}$ $_{tootity}$ $_{too.}$

Rooty $^{too.}$ Rooty $^{too.}$ Rooty $^{too-oo-oo.}$

And Gamboy, who was just passing him as he blew, started and smiled in spite of herself, and ran as best she could in her narrow dress to Violet and kissed her on the lips. But then the sound of the trumpet died away out of her ears, and she fell back ashamed of herself, glowering at everybody near her, and walked on in moody silence at the tail of the procession.

But when they reached the Castle, there was still another surprise in store for them. For the old King came up to the Prince and suddenly fell on his knees before him, offering him the hilt of his sword and saying:

"Homage to King Courtesy and Queen Violet!" Then Violet, who could not bear to see her father akneel, put her arms round his neck and raised him up, whereupon he explained that he and the Queen had decided that they were too old and too tired to reign any more, and they wished King Courtesy and his wife to govern the realm from now onwards. So Courtesy humbly thanked the old King for his kindness and vowed he would strive to be worthy of so great an honour. He and Violet took the oath there and then, and, as they mounted the throne, everybody in the Castle shouted aloud with one great shout:

"Long live King Courtesy and Queen Violet!" till the old stone walls echoed to the sound. And, as they mounted the throne, the Silver Trumpet rang out again, high above the shouting and the din:

$$\text{Rooty}^{\text{tootity}^{\text{tootity}^{\text{tootity}^{\text{tootity}^{\text{too.}}}}} \text{Too}_{\text{tootity}_{\text{tootity}_{\text{tootity}_{\text{too.}}}}}}$$

$$\text{Rooty}^{\text{too.}} \text{Rooty}^{\text{too.}} \text{Rooty}^{\text{too-oo-oo.}}$$

and then died slowly away, while Princess Gamboy walked, as in a dream, to the foot of the throne and bowed her head, doing homage to the King and to her sister, the Queen.

That night lights blazed from every window in the Castle, so that far away on the hills the shepherds, gathered around their fires, saw three unbroken rows of little twinkling lights like stars. And they took off their caps, crying:

"Long live the King and Queen!"

Nor did they know that it was a new King and Queen they were hailing.

But inside the Castle a great ball was afoot, with Japanese lanterns in the courtyard, and strawberries and peacocks for supper, and the Great Throne Hall blazing with candles. All the while the Little Fat Podger danced madly in and out of the throng, leaping higher and higher: "Up — up — up — and *again!*" he shrieked and turned two somersaults in the air, because Violet was happy. Nor was the new Queen herself too dignified to dance a little dance of her own in the centre of the hall, while everybody looked on. And when she had finished everyone applauded clamorously, not because she was Queen, but because she danced like a leaf in the wind. Everyone, that is, except Princess Gamboy. She sat alone and aloof at a corner of the supper-table, eating, eating, eating, and drinking, drinking, drinking. She had not even changed her clothes. And all the time she grew more and more jealous of the Prince and spiteful towards everybody; for this was not the kind of music that made her dream.

PART II

CHAPTER V

A YEAR SLIPPED by. The young King and Queen lived all that time in almost perfect happiness, for there was nothing now to mar their joy except Gamboy's tantrums. And though these were growing more frequent and more violent, yet they gave less trouble than before, because, now Courtesy was King, he took the law into his own hands and refused to let her come into the Presence unless she would behave herself. Violet agreed to this with great reluctance. She saw that it was necessary, but the coolness between herself and Gamboy was an increasing load of sorrow about her heart, a load which she could still feel in the midst of all her happiness, and one of which she longed to rid herself.

But what of the Silver Trumpet? Would not that serve to soften her sister's heart and to bring them together again, at least for an hour? Alas, it was lost! It had never been seen since the night of the wedding. On that night Queen Violet had asked the King to give it to her to play with. He had refused at first, for when he left home his Father had bidden him never, never to part with it, no, not even to save his life. But when he told Violet this, she only laughed and pouted a little, saying:

"Pooh, sir, you have small faith in our happiness, if you think it hangs on such a toy. Keep your old trumpet!"

She was merry with jest and dancing and meant small harm; yet Courtesy, who had never heard her speak so before, was troubled inwardly and felt his heart ache for a moment, as though he were alone. So, to ease his little pain, he gave it to her with a forced smile, saying:

"Guard it well, then, and at night see you keep it under lock and key."

Whereupon she took it and tossed it up like a ball for joy, but that very night left it lying on a couch in the Throne Hall. And when she woke in the middle of the night and remembered what she had done, she was sorry, but she would not trouble to go and put it away. For it seemed to her then that nothing could ever make her unhappy again, and that she and the King had no need to be careful of anything.

And now nobody knew where it was. Nobody? Yes, one person knew: Princess Gamboy. She had found it in the Throne Hall early the next morning, and taken and hidden it in an old disused loft above the stables. Princess Gamboy had come to hate and fear the strange power which that trumpet had over her. She was too proud, you see, to surrender to anything except her own self-will. And the thought of the new King everlastingly blowing his own trumpet drove her hopping mad.

But there were the five musicians with their five fiddles. Why could not they be brought in to make life more smooth at the Castle? Surely the King had not forgotten that wonderful moonlit evening in the West Corner of the Queen's Garden? No, he had not forgotten it, but (how sad it is to tell!) all was not well in the land over which King Courtesy ruled. Last year's harvest had failed, and his subjects were growing very poor. There would have been a famine in the cold winter, and all the little children would have starved or frozen to death, if the King had not sent abroad to the neighbouring countries to buy grain and fuel for his subjects. But the rich merchants of the neighbouring countries would not yield up their grain and their coal except for money. Consequently the King's Treasury grew emptier and emptier, the musicians had to be dismissed, and the King and Queen, although they lived in a great Castle, were very, very poor. In the evenings, while King Courtesy was racking his brains for ways and means to relieve the distress, the Queen would sit by the fire (such a small one!) mending up his old socks and turning his old clothes inside out to make them look like new. And this was a great hardship to the King, who until that year had always been given a new pair of socks every day. For the hardest of all trials in this world is to have to do without something you have been accustomed to all your life, and just at first I believe it was very nearly as hard for the King to do without his socks as it was for the poor people to do without their fires. But he knew, all the same, that fires were very much more important than new socks, so he said nothing about it to anyone.

Yet even this was not the saddest part of the story, for the people, in spite of all their King's efforts to help them, in spite of his empty Treasury and his tired, white face, began to growl and complain and even to threaten. They had never had a famine before, they said, and they had never had a King Courtesy before; therefore the one must be because of the other. Moreover there were many ill-natured people going about the land, who stirred up and increased this hatred as much as they could. And in particular there was one woman, whose fame soon spread abroad, because in that country it was not usual for women to get up and address a crowd.

"Citizens," she would cry, standing on a tub in the market-place, "fellow citizens, we've had enough of this! What happened last night? What will happen again tonight?" and she would pause, as though waiting for a reply. Then, as there was none, she would reply herself: "Why this will happen — some of us will be cold. Some of us will be frozen! ALL OF US WILL BE HUNGRY!"

And from the crowd of listeners would come a loud growl of assent. Then she would raise one accusing arm and sweep it round in the direction of Mountainy Castle with its rows of blazing windows: "Are the people in *there* cold? Are *they* hungry?" she would ask fiercely, and the crowd would raise its voice as one man and thunder out an indignant

"No!"

till the market-place rang again with the noise. When she had finished her speech, the people would gather into knots and talk in low voices, threatening to march up to the Castle and drag the King from his bed and kill him, while all the time, if they had only known, the poor man sat shivering in his fireless study signing papers, interviewing farmers, and devising schemes for the distribution of food and fuel to his subjects. But in the end they always decided to stay at home; for however much, in their ignorance, they had begun to hate King Courtesy, they still loved Queen Violet far too well; they had all loved her devotedly ever since she was a child. So for the present the King and Queen were safe.

One night the Queen lay in bed very ill, and beside her in the bed lay a tiny little daughter, two days old. The Physicians had spoken gravely to the King, telling him that the young Queen-mother must be kept absolutely quiet for a long time, as the slightest shock now might cause her death. Her death! The poor King was distracted with anxiety, but his Counsellors told him that he must not allow it to appear in his face, as the people were so discontented that they feared a revolution if it was known that the Queen lay in danger. "They would be certain," said the Counsellors, "to blame Your Majesty for it." This made King Courtesy very sorrowful, for he loved his subjects dearly and would have given his life for them. But what could he do? "Moreover," said the Counsellors, "Your Majesty would be wise to order every room in the Castle to be lit up tonight, so that the people down in the City and the shepherds far

away on the snow-covered hills may see the lights and be persuaded that all is well in Mountainy Castle." Then the King gave orders accordingly, and the lights blazed forth from the windows into the dark night.

But down in the City the same wicked woman, who had stirred the people up before, was speaking again:

"Look at those lights," she cried, pointing to the Castle: "nobody is cold in *there*; nobody starves *there*; big fires blaze all day on the hearths of empty rooms, burning up the coal that might be warming your wives and children; the tables in there are loaded with peacocks' breasts, while you are left to starve!" and the hungry men, shivering in the freezing east wind, their wet feet numbed by the snow about their boots, did not stop to ask if the woman were speaking the truth. Is it any wonder?

Nobody knew who she was or where she lived. Only one night a man had sworn that he saw her disappear into the Castle itself. That was strange. Tonight, too, she seemed to make off in that direction.

"She has gone to set fire to the Castle," suggested a young man in fun.

"She has gone to set fire to the Castle," shouted his neighbour.

"She has gone to set fire to the Castle. She has gone to set fire to the Castle," cried everybody, and everybody, except the young man who had suggested it, believed that it was true; for people will believe almost anything when people are excited and hungry enough.

"Stop her!" cried one.

"No!" said another.

"Yes!" shouted a third.

"What about Queen Violet?" cried another. "Are we going to let her be burnt alive?"

"No!"

"No!"

"No!"

"No!"

came the shouts from all sides, and everybody began talking at once at the top of everybody's voice. At last they decided that they would march to the Castle in procession, with flaring torches to show them the way, to rescue Queen Violet when the Castle was set on fire. But Princess Gamboy and the King, they said, they would leave to burn to death. Then they thought what a fine big blaze the burning Castle would make, and of the red glare that would go up into the sky, and their hearts grew warm within them as though they had drunk brandy. Half-an-hour later the procession started off; some of the men carried pitchforks and some axes, and their red faces peeped from the black night beneath the glare of the flaring torches. And as they marched they sang this song:

> "Left right, left right,
>   No more flour in the sack —
> Left right, left right,
>   No more coal on the stack —
> But we're going to get warm tonight,
>   My Boys,
>   Before we all come back."

"Do you see the flames bursting out?" said one.

"Look how the roof is smoking already!" cried his neighbour. But they only thought they had seen these things, because they wanted to see them.

"Ah," said a third, "I wonder how the woman got into the Castle. It is well guarded, neighbours, very well guarded."

"And I wonder who she is," said a fourth. They did not know that it was Princess Gamboy herself who had been speaking to them half-an-hour ago, and who had now gone back into the Castle simply because she lived there. You see, as she grew wickeder and wickeder, she had grown more cunning too, and she had taken to disguising herself and going out to try and stir up rebellion against her brother-in-law, the King, whom she hated so much. Many a time she had tried to tell the citizens how Violet lay ill, knowing that this, which was true, would inflame them against the King more than all the lies she could invent. But somehow the words stuck in her throat; she dreaded the outburst of indignation which would follow, for it would remind her of the great love which the people bore to her sister. Princess Gamboy still loved Violet more than she loved anything else in the world. But that was so little that even her love for Violet had become a kind of hatred. So she said nothing about her when she spoke to the citizens. And then, you see, she didn't want them to attack the Castle, because she lived in it herself. Besides, she had another plan on foot for satisfying her ugly jealousy of the King and Queen. She was hurrying back now to see if it had been successful.

She did not know, as she crept into the Castle, that the citizens were marching with their torches up the hill. She had heard a low, strange noise like the buzzing of gnats in the distance, and wondered for a moment what it was. That was all. But if she had listened very carefully she might have heard low, like the angry murmur of the sea, but getting steadily louder and louder:

"Left right, left right,
        No more flour in the sack —
Left right, left right,
        No more coal on the stack —
But we're going to get warm tonight,
        My Boys,
        Before we all come back."

CHAPTER VI

BUT WHAT HAD been happening inside the Castle all the time Gamboy was making her speech and the citizens were preparing to march? For many days past the Little Fat Podger had been striving hard to lighten the King's load of sorrow by jesting and dancing before him in the most ludicrous manner he could devise. Since Courtesy was now King, it was the Dwarf's duty, as Curator of the Royal Dump, to try to make him laugh, for his official task was to cure the King's megrims. And as he loved his new master even more than his old one, and could not bear to see him unhappy, he tried all the harder to do his duty well; but it was very uphill work.

Now the Dwarf had a little workshop, right at the top of a high round turret, and there he made all his own clothes and furniture; for no tailor would make a suit of clothes small enough for the Little Fat Podger, and no carpenter could make a tiny enough wash-stand. So he made them all himself. But he was so neat and tricksy with his fingers that he could make all sorts of things besides ordinary clothes and furniture. In addition to the little red suits of clothes which he wore every day, he used to make wonderful costumes and machines to dance in. He had cloth-covered wooden frameworks, some of which were like birds, some like fish, and some like the different animals, but one in particular, all covered over with green, with a wonderful attachment of wooden laths and steel springs, which was like a grasshopper. He would get into this framework and with the help of the wooden laths and steel springs, which were covered to look like a grasshopper's legs, he would perform the most ridiculous jigs that you ever saw. In happier days King Courtesy had been known to fall down weeping with laughter at the mere sight of it, but of late he had watched the Dwarf executing his wildest fandangos and had not even smiled. He was very unhappy indeed.

The poor Dwarf did not know what to do, and when he saw that the King took no notice of him he began to pine and mope. Everybody always laughed at him, but the only people he really *liked* to laugh were Courtesy and Violet and Violet's Father and Mother, who were getting too old now to laugh very much. He would eat no food and spent most of the day sitting in his little workshop, staring idly at his tools, with the tears trickling down his coat. Alas, this went on for a whole month, and the Little Fat Podger grew so thin that he ought to have been called the Little Thin Podger. But one evening he was looking vacantly out of the window when he saw the King pacing up and down the garden underneath. Suddenly he stopped in his walk and burst out laughing. The Little Fat Podger could not believe his eyes: he craned out of the window to see what it could be that had made his gloomy master smile, and what was his surprise to see that it was nothing more than a clumsy great green toad, which had lolloped into the middle of the garden path and sat there looking at the King without taking the slightest trouble to get out of his way. The Dwarf stood at the

window looking out at the King, and the King stood in the garden looking at the toad. The King laughed. The Dwarf gaped. There they stood stock-still, till the toad gathered itself together and flumped heavily to the side of the path.

Lollopy-lump, lollopy-lump, lollopy-lump! went the toad.

The King went on his way.

Up jumped the Dwarf and flew to his bench. Off came his coat, and in two minutes he was working furiously, surrounded by the greatest pudder that was ever seen — tools of every shape and size, gold paint, green paint, black paint, varnish, laths, steel springs, elastic bands, glass eyes, electric bulbs, cranks, pulleys, and the insides of seven clockwork engines.

"Never say die till you're dead!" he whistled, as he planed away at one of the best and smoothest of his stock of laths, and the plane was so sharp and the wood so soft and firm that it was like paring a slab of cheese. He worked on without stopping for two days and nights, and all that time he ate nothing but bananas. Every half-hour he would pause for a minute to eat a banana, so that by the end of the second day he had eaten ninety-six bananas. But he wasn't ill. And on the evening of the second day there in the corner of his workshop, striped with glossy black and green and gold, and shining-new with varnish, stood a beautiful mechanical toad, ten times larger than life. All four legs could be worked from the inside by springs, and the eyes were two bulging bulbs, which could be lit up by means of a little electric switch inside the body. It was lovely. The Little Fat Podger ate four more bananas and drank a glass of port; then in he jumped and began to lollop down the winding stair to look for the King and make him laugh.

Lollopy-lump, lollopy-lump, lollopy-lump.

On the way he passed a scullery-maid, and she screamed and ran away for fright, but the Little Fat Podger didn't hear this because in his hurry he had forgotten to make ear-holes in his machine.

Now this was the very afternoon of the day on which Princess Gamboy went down into the City, all of which you have already heard about. What you haven't heard is that, just as she was starting out, she had met the Dwarf inside his toad. But *she* wasn't frightened — not she. And it was then that she suddenly thought of her plan. It was a very cruel plan.

She called to the Dwarf; but he didn't hear, because he had forgotten to make ear-holes. So she called again. But still he didn't hear, — he just went lolloping on, as though nobody was there. Then she ran after him and thumped on the toad's wooden back, calling out:

"Little Fat Podger! Little Fat Podger!"

This time he could just hear, but he was so muffled up in his machine that he could not tell whose voice it was.

"Yes?" he shouted.

"Will you take this note to Queen Violet for me?" cried Gamboy.

"Very well," called the obliging little fellow. "Put it under me!"

So Princess Gamboy took a piece of paper from her purse, folded it up, and scribbled "V. R." on it, which stood for *Violetta Regina*, which is Latin for Queen Violet, and she thrust it underneath the machine, and the Dwarf took it.

But there was nothing written inside the piece of paper.

The Little Fat Podger gave up looking for the King, however, and trundled off to Violet's room with the note. The Queen was in bed with her tiny little daughter, alone in the dark. She was very pale and thin. When the Dwarf knocked at the door, she called out in a weak voice:

"Come in!"

Of course the Dwarf didn't hear this, but he opened the door very gently and went in without waiting for an answer. He knew the Queen wouldn't mind.

Shut up in his workshop for two whole days, he had not heard of the Physicians' orders that Violet was to be kept very quiet. Nor did he know anything about the tiny little daughter, so he opened the door very gently and went in.

Far away, down in the City, Princess Gamboy on her tub was pointing scornfully to the brilliantly-lit Castle, and all the citizens were thinking, "How happy everybody must be in the Castle! I expect there is dancing going on behind those bright windows. How different from all *our* misery!"

But now Queen Violet looked from her bed and saw a great green toad coming in at the door with bulging eyes that shone right across the dark room. And she was very ill, and she raised herself up in bed and uttered one loud scream of terror and fell back dead.

But the Dwarf didn't hear her scream, because he had forgotten to make ear-holes.

And he thought to himself: "Now I am here, I will try and cheer the Queen up a little." So he worked the springs and switched the lights on and off and flopped clumsily up and down the room, chuckling to himself to think how the Queen must be laughing, though he couldn't hear it, and how much better she would be for it afterwards. And the little two-day-old baby in the bed looked on all the time with wide, wide eyes, not knowing at all what was happening, but much too young to feel frightened. But then the Dwarf happened to turn the toad's electric eyes in the direction of the bed. They shone full on the Queen's pale face. He saw what had happened.

Crash! He had jumped through the side of his machine, like a circus-rider piercing a paper hoop, and was kneeling by the bedside, chafing the Queen's hands and imploring her to answer him. But she said nothing. And then the Little Fat Podger began to weep, because he had killed his mistress.

This was Princess Gamboy's plan, you see.

Soon the Physicians came in to see how Queen Violet was. And when they saw what had happened, they sent for the King. But I will not try and tell you what King Courtesy felt when he came into that bedroom. Of course everybody thought it was the Dwarf's fault, and the King at once ordered him to be arrested. But the poor little Dwarf didn't care at all what they thought of him. He only wanted so badly to explain to Queen Violet that he hadn't *meant* to frighten her.

"Mistress! Mistress!" he kept saying, while they put handcuffs on him and took him away, "Oh, mistress, you do understand, don't you?"

But of course Violet didn't understand, because she couldn't hear.

And now a noise was heard outside the castle wall. It was the mob of citizens who had at last arrived at the top of the hill:

"No more flour in the sack"

they sang. And they beat upon the Castle gate with their pitchforks and axes, crying, "Let us in, let us in!"

The King did not know what it was; but when he had listened to them out of the window for a little, he understood, and himself went quietly downstairs and alone across the courtyard to open the gates. As soon as the gate began to creak ajar, the foremost among them made a rush to get in, but when they saw the King, they were abashed and fell back. Yet the people behind still pressed them forward.

"Where is Queen Violet?" they cried. "We have come to save her."

And then the King began to speak to them, and he spoke in the same funny polite voice in which he had spoken to Violet when he first met her in the West Corner of the Queen's Garden.

"Sirs," he said, "I fear your zeal outruns your discretion. Nevertheless it is now my painful duty to inform you that your kindness arrives too late. The lady is dead, you see — Dead — no doubt you have heard the word before. And now, sirs, I perceive

animosity in your looks. If anyone would care to fillip me up a little with an axe or a pitchfork — what can I say? I am his King and therefore entirely at his service." And King Courtesy bared and bowed his neck, waiting for some one of his subjects to come at him and strike off his head.

But not one of the crowd made a move. The anger suddenly died out of them when they thought of their beloved Queen lying white and cold in her bed in the Castle. Gradually they fell back, and one by one slunk away down the hill towards their homes.

"Goodnight, sirs," called out the King through his nose. "Oh, goodnight, I'm sure!" and he closed the Castle gate.

But when he had shut the gate and was alone, his queer manner suddenly changed. His head hung down, his shoulders began to droop, his knees bent beneath him, and he looked like an old, old man.

CHAPTER VII

THERE WAS NO bacon at little Princess Lily's christening. Princess Lily was the name of Violet's tiny little daughter, who was now growing larger and larger every day. But the christening was a very quiet affair, with no breakfast and no guests, because the King would have it so. After he had sent the citizens back to their homes on the night the Queen died, the King had walked straight to his private study and locked himself in. He had refused to see anybody or to take any interest in affairs of State. He would not even see his little daughter or give orders as to what was to be done with her. He was too full of hopeless grief to be able to think of anything but Violet, Violet, Violet. All day long and all night the thought of her filled his mind. Where was she? He could not believe that she would not soon knock gently on the door and come in.

Only once did he send for anybody to come to his chamber. And that was on the second day after he had entered it, when he sounded a bell and sent a page for the Lord High Teller of the Other from Which, who had recently been appointed Lord Chancellor. The new Lord Chancellor appeared, and the King asked him:

"When does the trial of my Dwarf fall due?" He would not use the name "Little Fat Podger," because that was a funny little name.

"Sire," said the Lord Chancellor, "it falls due tomorrow, but it will not take place."

"How!" exclaimed the King, "are my orders disobeyed, then?"

"Sire," said the Lord Chancellor, "I regret to say that the Dwarf passed away this morning in gaol." And he told the King how the shock had been too much for the Little Fat Podger. Weak as he was already, from having eaten nothing for a whole month except a hundred bananas, he quickly grew weaker still, and never recovered himself enough even to understand that he was in gaol awaiting trial for Murder and High Treason. He had talked continually, said his gaoler, of the dreadful mistake he had made, and was troubled because Violet had not answered when he tried to explain to her. Yet he seemed, as the time went by, to grow calmer and calmer, until this morning (and the Lord Chancellor mournfully repeated the words he had used before) he had "passed quietly away".

But the King, when he heard this, only frowned and commanded that the Dwarf should be buried outside the common burying-ground, alone and with no inscription on his tomb, and that no man should speak his name under penalty of death. For he knew nothing of Princess Gamboy's plan, and believed, as was to be expected, that the Dwarf had deliberately killed his mistress. So nobody knew what had happened, except Princess Gamboy, and though keeping quiet was not one of her habits, she kept very quiet about this.

For six months little Princess Lily lived with her Grandfather and Grandmother. They were stricken with grief for their favourite daughter and glad to have a little baby to look after. But after six months King Courtesy began to recover himself like a man and strove to take an interest in the government of his country. He no longer lived locked in his study, but went about the Castle in the old way, though at first everything he came to reminded him of the Queen, and gave him a great stab of pain in the heart, and made him want to sit down. He never went near the West Corner of the Queen's Garden.

But he soon became very fond of his little daughter, the Princess Lily. She, too, reminded him of Violet, but somehow that did not seem to hurt in the same way. As she grew up, she grew more and more beautiful, and it was soon plain that when she became a lady she would be even more beautiful than Violet herself had been. You see, she had no twin, no Gamboy, with whose looks her own were magically linked. And as her heart was like Violet's and not like Gamboy's, her face blossomed into what Violet's face would have been but for Gamboy's wrinkles and old Miss Thomson's queer spell. Very soon — even before she was a year old — she and her father became the closest companions. Wherever he went, he would take her with him, perched on his shoulder or in a little sling at his side, and all the time he would talk and talk to her — long before she could understand what he was saying. As soon as she grew more sturdy on her pins, the King was very anxious that she should learn to dance. For now that the Little Fat Podger and the Queen were both gone, there was nobody at all to dance to him. And then a very strange thing happened.

It was discovered that she could dance most beautifully without being taught a step!

"Quite *beautifully*, my dear!" said all the *Amalgamated Princesses* who came to the Castle to see Princess Gamboy, and who didn't really care for dancing in the least but were much too silly to say so and have done with it. So for a long time Princess Lily and the King were very happy together, at least she was very happy and he was not so sad. Every evening they would sit together in his study, little Lily and her Father, and he would take her on his knee and read to her all the wise and lovely things written by the men who lived a long time ago, and, when they were tired of this, Princess Lily would get up and go into the light of the lamp and dance a solemn little dance of her own making, and the King would clap his hands with delight and look quite young again. She had a way of making little dresses for herself to dance in, you know, and one evening she suddenly appeared to the King in a papery frock all of russet-brown and danced wildly and oh so lightly up and down the great room with her hair streaming out behind, as though there were a strong wind blowing. "That was my Leaf Dance," she cried out, as she ran back to her Father's knee. But she found there were tears in his eyes and great lines of sorrow down his face, for he remembered how his Queen, too, had used to dance like a leaf in the wind. So she never wore that dress or danced that dance again, the dance in which she pretended to be a brown autumn leaf, blown along by the jolly wind. But she made other dresses and danced other dances, a Spring Dance, all in green, a Summer Dance, and a Winter Dance, in white like a

snow-flake. And sometimes, while the King was reading to Lily beside the shaded lamp, or Lily was dancing to the King beneath the hanging one, Princess Gamboy, pretending some errand or other, would open the door and come into the room. She would stand just inside the door looking at them, and then, if the King was reading, she would say:

"Stuff!"

or if little Lily was dancing, she would say:

"Tsch!"

after which she would turn on her heel and go out, slamming the door. At such times Princess Lily would ask, "What is the matter with Aunt Gamboy?" And King Courtesy would reply meekly, "I don't know, my dear," and fall silent with a cloud over his eyes. For since the Queen's death he had never had the heart to be angry with Gamboy. He knew how much Violet had loved her, and anything Violet had loved was precious to him. Therefore he always tried his hardest to please her, although the only thanks he received would be

"Stuff!"

or

"Tsch!"

All the same Aunt Gamboy (she was *Aunt* Gamboy now) had given up trying to stir rebellion among the King's subjects. That was something. But whether this was out of gratitude to the King for his gentleness or because she had another little plan of her own, you must guess for yourself.

Luckily the harvests had been good since the dreadful winter when the citizens had marched up to the Castle on the cold night of Queen Violet's death, so that they were happy and contented. Moreover they were sensible citizens and soon began to discover what a wise, unselfish ruler their King really was. And gradually they came to love him nearly as fondly as they had once loved the Queen.

CHAPTER VIII

WHEN PRINCESS LILY was between seven and eight years old, a curious thing happened in Mountainy Castle. It was all the more remarkable because, if there ever was anybody in the world who could be relied upon to behave in exactly the same way upon all occasions, morning and evening, year in year out, Sundays and Christmas Day included, that body was Aunt Gamboy. You always knew just what she was going to wear, just what she was going to do, and just what she was going to say; for all you needed to do was to think carefully as she opened the door or her mouth, what thing you most hoped she wouldn't wear, do, and say. And then she wore, did, and said it.

But now, very slowly as it seemed, she began to change.

She would still snap the heads off the Castle servants with her sharp tongue, she would still set the Lord Chamberlain and the Lord High Teller of the Other from Which (who had lately received the honourable title of Lord Tullywich) and all the other noble lords of the land by the ears with some ill-judged remark, she would still pore for hours over her black-bound book called *Excerpta*, and she would still feed the *Amalgamated Princesses* on aerated bread and desiccated cocoanut, but nevertheless there *was* a change. And with Aunt Gamboy any sort of change at all, even the tiniest one, was startling enough to everyone who knew her. She put on different clothes. She began to tie her hair with one piece of ribbon instead of three pieces of string. If she was talking to the King, or if she was talking to anyone else and the King was within hearing, her voice would grow a little softer and her tongue a little less sharp. Sometimes she was almost kind to him, on one occasion she even said "Thank you" instead of "Stuff!" and the next night she filled his hot-water bottle from her own kettle.

No doubt she had noticed what everyone else in the Castle had begun to see — that King Courtesy, in spite of little Lily and her pretty pranks, was a sad and lonely man. As he grew older and more tired he seemed to miss the Queen more and more, and at night, when his work was over and he sat in the firelight, he would sometimes fancy she was there beside him, till one of the flames, leaping higher than before, would light up all the room and remind him that he was alone. This would always be long after Princess Lily had gone to bed. At such times he would sit by the hearth far on into the night, his elbows upon his knees and his chin upon his hands, gazing, gazing into the fire, until it turned grey and then black and he was shivery with cold. Then he would trudge wearily up to bed and lie awake till morning, wondering why he had been born.

No doubt Aunt Gamboy had noticed all this.

CHAPTER IX

ONE BLOWING AUTUMN afternoon the King was out walking alone with Princess Lily. He was plodding slowly over the damp fields and footpaths of his demesne, with little Lily's small hand gripped tight in his big one and little Lily's little legs hurrying along beside his large ones, two steps to one. They were talking happily together of this, that, and the other, and watching the round sun putting on his gorgeous red clothes before he went to bed. But when silence fell between them, the King began to puzzle to himself over the strange alteration in Aunt Gamboy's behaviour and he could not help thinking how pleasant it would be, when the walk was over, to come back to the Castle and find her waiting with the China tea made ready and the Royal Slippers warming by the fire; for she had taken lately to drinking tea with him. But Princess Lily had a bright little picture in *her* head of the warm Nursery, with the blinds drawn and the fire flickering away behind the guard, and Indian tea and thick bread and butter with the Royal Nurse. "How nice it will be," she thought, "not to have that horrid Aunt Gamboy fussing in and out, making draughts and banging the door. She always stays downstairs now, thank goodness!"

They walked on in silence. Suddenly Princess Lily stopped dead, threw up her hands, and screamed a great scream. Her eyes and her mouth opened wider and wider and rounder and rounder; once, twice, three times she screamed aloud. Then she raised herself up on tiptoe and down she plopped backwards in a dead faint. The poor King was astonished. He snatched her up in his arms and turned to see what it could be that had frightened her so much. He looked all round, but there was nobody in sight. He looked all round again. Still he saw nothing. He looked all round *again*. And then he threw back his head and began to laugh. For lolloping along by the side of the path, believe me, in the clumsiest and most ridiculous way imaginable, was a great grey-green toad.

Lollopy-lump, lollopy-lump, lollopy-lump!

But then the King suddenly understood that it was this which had frightened poor little Lily and sent her off a-fainting. He stopped laughing and looked very gravely at his daughter lying in his arms. And now she slowly opened her eyes and asked wonderingly where she was and what had happened.

"You are out for a walk with your Father and you have just seen a toad," said the King.

"What is a toad?" asked Lily.

And then King Courtesy (and you will remember that although he was not very clever he was very wise) thought for a moment and, when he had thought, he looked bang into Princess Lily's eyes and said:

"Are you a brave little Princess?"

"Yes," said Lily, "I think so."

The King put her on her feet and, taking her hand in his, said:

"Now you are quite safe, and you know there is nothing to be frightened of when you are with me, don't you?"

"Yes, Your Majesty," said little Lily.

"You are quite sure?"

"Yes, Father."

"Very well. *That* is a toad!" said the King, pointing to it and watching his daughter to see what would happen. Well, her eyes began to open wider and wider and her mouth to grow rounder and rounder and she was just going to scream again; but the King pressed her hand tight, to remind her that he was there, and this time she did not faint, though she felt little trembles running up and down all over her like mice. She just stood shivering and shaking like a leaf hanging on the branch of a tree, when the wind blows it about, and she would not look at the great grey-green toad lolloping along in the ditch.

"Oh, Father, take me home, take me home!" she whimpered. So the King turned with her and walked towards home.

How queer, thought the King, as they walked home, that a thing which makes one person laugh should make another scream and shiver. He could not understand it. He did not remember the little two-day-old baby who only lay in a Queen's bed and watched with wide-open eyes the antics of that strange mechanical toad. Nor did Princess Lily herself remember it, for she had been so young then that her memory hadn't started. But somewhere inside her, somewhere behind those wide, wide eyes, the jumping toad with its electric glare and her Mother's loud scream in the dark had printed their mark, just as a picture is printed inside a picture-machine, though if you opened the machine you would see nothing.

This was the first time since then that she had seen a toad. Oh, if only she had listened to nobody but her Father! For now His Majesty began to explain, as they walked along, that there was nothing to be frightened of in a toad or indeed in any other of God's creatures — except lions and tigers.

"Only weak and silly people scream when they see mice and spiders and toads," he said: "all sensible people know that they are really just as beautiful as bees and butterflies and robins. But you must get to know them and you mustn't be frightened."

Then Princess Lily began to feel a little ashamed of herself. All the way home the King talked to her in this way and promised to help her to be brave and untrembly, telling her stories of the way in which other people had conquered their fears.

When they reached the Castle, Lily ran upstairs to the Royal Nursery for tea. She said nothing to her old Nurse about the toad, because she felt she would rather not speak of it to anyone. She only wanted to forget all about it very quickly.

King Courtesy opened the door of the Tea Hall and went in. He found Aunt Gamboy sitting behind a table waiting for him. She had put away her spectacles (indeed she hardly ever wore them now except in her own room) and she had left her black book upstairs (she hardly ever read it now except in her own room); and there she sat behind the table. How like the Queen she was! The King was beginning to notice this

more and more, and sometimes, when they sat alone
together in one of the rooms in the Castle, a great
peace would come to him and he would almost believe
that Violet was with him again. If he looked very hard
at Aunt Gamboy at these times, he fancied her face
changing under his very eyes; not the features
themselves, but the look on them seemed to slide and
change, to change like the shape of a cloud, until he
fell in a dream that his beloved Queen herself was
looking out at him through Gamboy's eyes. Then the
world and the Castle and the walls of the room would
all seem very shadowy and far-away, and he would
dream on, wondering what might be the difference
between life and death.

He sat down at the table:

"Such a curious thing happened this afternoon,
when we were out for a walk," he said.

"What was it, my dear?" said Gamboy.

Yes, Aunt Gamboy called the King "My dear"! So he
told her all that had happened, and of course she was
very surprised, and told the King that she couldn't
understand it at all. She quite agreed, she said, that
little Lily must be taught to conquer her silly fear. It
was not the thing, she said, for a Princess to be afraid.
She had never been afraid of toads, she said, or
anything else, and she would do her best to cure her
niece. That was the end of their talk on that matter.

But Aunt Gamboy knew more about toads than
anybody else in the country. She had read about them
in that black book of hers. There was a good deal of
magic in that book. And, of course, as it was a black
book, it was Black Magic. It was because she knew so

much about toads that she had sent the Little Fat Podger into her sister's room on the night he finished his machine and got inside it. She had known well enough what would happen. That was why she had done it. And since that night she had been reading, reading, reading. She had taken lately, as you know, to leaving her book upstairs, but she had not stopped reading it. When she was not smiling sweetly at the weary King or calling him "My dear", you would have found her, if you had looked, upstairs in her room, horn-rimmed spectacles on nose, poring over her book and reading about — toads.

"Oh dear! Here's that horrid Aunt Gamboy," thought Lily to herself as she heard Aunt Gamboy's footsteps coming upstairs to the Royal Nursery.

CHAPTER X

"WELL, MY DEAR," said Aunt Gamboy, closing the door behind her, "and did you have a nice walk?"

It was the first time Aunt Gamboy had ever called her niece "My dear". Lily couldn't help feeling a little proud, because that was what the *Amalgamated Princesses* called each other, and though she didn't like those ladies very much, they *were* grown up. They called each other "*My* dears" and children "*Little* dears". Lily had always hated being called "Little dear". So when Aunt Gamboy called her "My dear", she was very glad. You see, the *Amalgamated Princesses* was a society of gentlewomen from the neighbouring kingdoms, who met together once a month at Mountainy Castle to talk. They had all been Princesses at one time of their lives but had been banished from their countries for disobeying regulations. Some of them had tied their hair up before they were twenty-one years old, some of them had neglected to keep it well keemed, some of them had worn the wrong clothes, and some of them had broken other laws of which you have not heard. But they were all alike in this, that they were no longer Princesses. That was why they called themselves the *Amalgamated Princesses*. And they all acknowledged Aunt Gamboy, who really was a Princess, as their leader. So Lily knew that if Aunt Gamboy called her

"My dear", all these ladies would be sure to call her
"My dear" too, and she would no longer have to bear
their horrid patronage. That was why, although she
had been so cross when she first heard Aunt Gamboy's
step on the stair, she turned to her now with a
pleasant smile and said:

"Yes, thank you, Aunt."

Aunt Gamboy sat down.

"What nasty weather we are having!" she said.
Princess Lily felt prouder than ever, for though her
Aunt had often *talked* to her before, she had never
conversed with her like this. She sat up straight and
patted her hair.

"Yes, isn't it nasty?" she said primly. "Won't you
have some tea?"

"I've already had some, thank you, my dear," said
Aunt Gamboy, smirking to herself at the success of her
little plan. And so the conversation went on, and all
the time it was more like two Aunts conversing
together than an Aunt talking to a niece. After a time
a little page-boy came in and cleared up the tea things.
Then he swept the Royal hearth, drew the curtains,
and went away leaving Princess Lily and Aunt
Gamboy sitting opposite each other over the bright,
clean fire. They sat watching the flames in silence,
and Princess Lily forgot all about the toad and only
thought how nice it was to be quiet and peaceful and
grown up, and how kind Aunt Gamboy was when you
really got to know her.

The clock ticked the silence away.

A rustling sound, a mouse in the wainscot, or
perhaps somebody scraping a chair in the room below;

and behold, Aunt Gamboy gave a little tittering scream, yes she did, and hopped up on to her chair switching her skirts about her knees. What was the matter? Little Lily's heart went thump, thump.

"Why, Aunt," she cried, trembling to see her Aunt tremble so, "whatever is the matter?"

But Aunt Gamboy was panting (so it seemed to her niece) for want of breath. She began to gasp words out:

"I-h-thought-h-it-h-might-h-be-h-a-T — "

But then her teeth chattered, clack, clack, clack, like Spanish castanets, so loudly that she could not utter the last word at all. Now Lily had never looked inside her Aunt's black book. If she had, she might have seen a paragraph beginning:

TEETH: Chatter, how to make (*a*) Others.
(*b*) Own.

And she would have noticed that (*b*) was underlined, which would have been a very good thing for her. But, as it was, *her* teeth began to chatter too, for there is nothing more terrifying than to see someone else terrified, and she, too, jumped up on her chair and snatched at her skirts, though without knowing why. So there they stood, trembling and staring at each other from two chairs on either side of the fireplace.

Soon, however, Aunt Gamboy grew calmer. She climbed down and sat in her chair once more. So Princess Lily climbed down too, and again she asked her Aunt what was the matter. For a long time Aunt Gamboy made no reply. Then at last she went to Princess Lily and, throwing her arms round her neck, wept on her shoulder.

"Oh, my dear," she cried, shuddering, "I thought I heard a T — " and she gulped a sob down and would not speak the word. Then suddenly it came into Lily's mind that the thing her Aunt was so frightened of, the word she could not speak, was "Toad". As the tide rushes into a pool of sand, rushed back to her now the memory of her afternoon's walk and of the great grey-green shining thing with its bulging eyes. In a moment she became even more trembly than Aunt Gamboy. She shivered and shook so that the chair rattled beneath her, and her eyes opened themselves wide and stared as they had stared only once before, when she was a baby two days old. Her breath came faster and faster. Aunt Gamboy unlocked her arms from her niece's neck and stood up. Whereat Princess Lily gave one long sigh and fell with her head over the arm of the chair, like a doll; and Aunt Gamboy, looking her up and down without moving, uttered the word

"Successful!"

Then she sat down in her chair again to wait. "Weak," she murmured to herself, "a weak child — easily upset. Hm — a weak child, a lonely father, and" (here Aunt Gamboy rose and looked at herself in the glass) "Princess Gamboy, at your service," she simpered, bowing to the image in the mirror, which bowed as politely back.

Little Lily, on her chair, began to stir her limbs. Aunt Gamboy arranged her face in front of the glass, knelt down beside her niece, and began to whisper to her the most pitiful words:

"My darling childie, are you better now?" she whispered. "Put your head in my lap, my sweet.

There, there, then!" And Princess Lily opened her eyes
and looked wonderingly up into her Aunt's eyes. Then,
when she saw who it was, a trustful little smile
spread over her face and she closed her eyes again
and pretended to sleep. Aunt Gamboy began to talk
to her.

"Are *you* afraid of Toads, Aunt?" said Lily, opening
her eyes.

"Hush, dear, don't think about it."

"Yes, but are you?"

"Hush, hush, there's a good child! There are not
many things your old Aunt is afraid of."

"Yes, but, tell me, are you afraid of Toads?"

"Hush!"

"Aunt!" said the little Princess, beginning to cry:
"You *are* afraid of them, you are, you are. Oh, what
are they? What will they do to me if they catch me?
Tell me!" And she began to shiver again. But Aunt
Gamboy, who had just promised the King to help his
daughter to conquer her fear, said nothing and looked
away. She is frightened, thought Lily; if she, who is so
strong and fearless, cannot protect me, then who will?
And she wept for loneliness and fell to trembling again
more than ever. Then she thought of her Father.

"Father told me there was nothing to fear," she
sobbed out.

Aunt Gamboy said nothing.

"Father told me there was nothing to fear," she cried
again.

"Yes, but — your Father — " said Aunt Gamboy and
stopped.

"Why should he tell it me if it wasn't true?"

" — is — " went on Aunt Gamboy slowly, as though she hadn't heard. She was thinking of something false to tell her niece.

"Oh, I'm so frightened. Need I sleep alone tonight?" wailed Lily.

" — a man," finished Aunt Gamboy, "Your Father is a man, my child, and doesn't understand."

"Oh, why not?" cried Lily miserably. "I am going to tell him at once and ask if I can sleep in the room next to his tonight," and she started running towards the door.

"Come here!" said Aunt Gamboy from her chair by the fire.

"No. I am going to find the King."

"Come here!"

"I want my Father!"

"Listen, Lily, do you love your Father?"

"Yes."

"Do you know that he is very tired and unhappy just now and very full of affairs? Are you going to trouble him still more and turn his hair grey? For shame! Besides, he is a man, and couldn't understand if you did tell him. He couldn't help you. If you love him, you will say nothing about it."

Poor little Lily was young enough to believe all this, to believe that it would be wrong to tell her own Father that she was trembly!

"I won't tell him, Aunt," she said. "May I come and sleep in the room next to yours tonight?"

"You're a good girl. Of course you may. And we'll both do everything we can to keep the — to keep them out. If we can't" (and she shrugged her shoulders), "we can't, — that is all." Saying which Aunt Gamboy turned and left the room.

"*If we can't, we can't*," the terrible words echoed in Princess Lily's ears. How she longed to tell her Father everything. She remembered how wisely he had spoken to her on the way home from their walk and how he had told her to fear none of God's creatures. Why, he had even laughed at the horrible thing, as if it was a joke. Perhaps it was a joke. How safe Lily would feel if she could hold his hand and tell him all about it. Surely it would be all right. She would do it. But no; for then she remembered her Aunt Gamboy's words. How dreadful, if she were really to turn her father's hair grey!

A cinder clicked in the grate, and Princess Lily started and remembered suddenly that she was alone in the room.

She had never feared to be alone before, but now she began to shiver and shake from head to foot. What was that noise? How tall Aunt Gamboy had looked just now standing on the chair — and how strange! What was that shadow moving on the wall? Princess Lily ran out of the room, turning her face away from the looking-glass as she passed, and fled downstairs to the Great Hall, where she could hear the Castle servants moving about. There she felt safer.

Meanwhile Aunt Gamboy was talking to the King in the Tea Hall:

"Yes," she said, "I've done my best to help the child. Poor little tot! I told her there was nothing whatever to be frightened at. I think she has got over it already. I am sure you will find she'll say no more about it to you. Best keep quiet about it yourself, my dear. By the way, in case she *should* feel at all nervous, I have arranged for her to sleep in the room next to mine tonight. She said she would feel quite, quite safe there — quite, *quite* safe."

And the King, who knew nothing of what had happened upstairs, was much moved and full of love for Aunt Gamboy because of her kindness in helping his daughter in her trouble. He looked at her as she sat with her eyes fixed modestly on the floor, and, when he had been gazing for a little, she raised her head and looked steadily back at him. Then it was that the King positively started because of her likeness to Violet. Her eyes seemed to grow larger and more transparent and to move nearer to him, and it was as though a voice spoke out of them saying "It is I, Violet, who am looking at you, my own darling: not dead, but hidden in here." And, as he looked, an agony of dreary longing sighed in the King's lonely heart, like a wind over the sea at night, and with it came once more the dream and filled all the room, till the world and the Castle and the walls of the room grew shadowy and far away, and only the Queen was near. He leaned his head over the table nearer to Gamboy's: "Most Gracious Lady," he began whispering to her, "pardon the intrusion — pardon the intrusion — pardon the intrusion — er — if I am something too forward in my address, you must believe that it is your beauty which has stolen my manners." "What a fool!" thought Aunt Gamboy, as she listened to what he was saying — "What a fool he is! But he is rich, and a King, and I would like a Prince to my son or a Princess to my daughter."

That night Princess Lily, lying in the room next to her Aunt's, dreamed a dream. She seemed to be standing amid long green grasses by the margin of a willowed pool, waiting for her Father. How happy she was; but suddenly the grass near her began to move, and she walked away, pretending not to hurry, for she knew something dreadful had seen her. As she came out on to the road, she looked back and saw a great green toad lolloping along behind her. She quickened her pace; the toad did the same. She broke into a run. Faster and faster lollopped on the toad, always drawing a little nearer, always staring at her with stony eyes. Oh dear, oh dear, how frightened she was in her dream! Princess Lily flew on and on towards the Palace and, looking back once, she saw that the toad had ceased lolloping and broken into a steady run, striding over the ground with long spidery legs. She was panting for breath. Would she reach home before her strength gave out? Ah, at last there was the door in front of her! She seized hold of the handle, but it had stuck fast and would not even rattle in her hand. She screamed "Help!" but no sound at all came out of her mouth, and she felt the toad's chill breath blowing the hair about her neck, as she flung herself on the door and discovered that it had been open all the time, only needing a push. She tried to slam it behind her in the animal's face, but it had caught on a hook in the wall and would not move. Sobbing for breath, she stumbled upstairs to her Aunt's room and found her standing stock still behind the bed, smiling. Princess Lily ran round the bed to her and tried to speak, but could not for want of breath.

Lollopy-lump, lollopy-lump, lollopy-lump!

Poor little Lily dreamed she heard the toad hoisting itself up the stairs the way she had come. She seized her Aunt by the dress and pointed to the door, but tall, thin Aunt Gamboy only stood stock still and smiled and smiled; yet Princess Lily knew somehow that she understood it all, though she would do nothing. In despair she rushed out of the other door and down Gamboy's own staircase to the King's study. If only she could get to her Father!

Lollopy-lump!

She heard the toad at the top of the stairs as she pushed open the study door. There, inside, was her Father standing with his arm in Aunt Gamboy's, and Lily never stopped to wonder how her Aunt had got there. "Father!" she shrieked (and this time her voice came), "the Toad, the Toad!" but His Majesty only burst out laughing, and when she called to him again she saw that he was very small and round like a little toy figure of indiarubber, and his head only came up to Gamboy's waist. He went on giggling, and Aunt Gamboy stood and smiled and smiled, nor did either of them seem to understand that the toad was even now pushing open the door behind her. She stood — in her dream — frozen with terror, watching her little father open his mouth wider and wider, and louder and louder grew his laughing till it grumbled and muttered round the whole room, and she woke up to find herself alone in the dark with a thunderstorm going on outside.

At first she lay still, not daring to move or make a sound, full of the dream, but then, remembering where she was, she called out through the door to her Aunt:

"Auntie, Auntie, are you there? I'm frightened." And Aunt Gamboy, lying awake next door and listening to the storm, heard little Lily call out to her; but she made no sound, as though she were asleep and hadn't heard, she made no sound. Then Lily cried out again:

"Auntie, Auntie," and again and again "Auntie, Auntie!" But Aunt Gamboy lay and smiled to herself in the dark and answered not a word. At last Lily felt ashamed of crying any more in case any other people in the Castle should hear her, and as she dared not get out of bed and find her way in the dark to her Aunt's room, she lay trembling and starting at every little creak of the woodwork and every rumbling echo of the thunder, until the window-pane turned grey. Then, when the dawn was come, she felt safer again and so tired that she turned over and went straight off to sleep. But in the morning she woke tossing and tossing in the throes of a high fever. And when someone came and stood by her bed, she thought in her delirium that the lady was her own dear Mother, of whose loving-kindness the King had so often spoken to her, and at once she held out both her hands to her, crying piteously:

"Oh Lady-Mother, my forehead is so hot!" hoping and hoping that her Mother would stoop and comfort it with her darling cool palms.

But of course Aunt Gamboy did nothing of the sort.

PART III

CHAPTER XI

"VERY WELL, THEN. Go! And never let me see your face again!"

It was the Court of Strenvaig, and old King Stren was speaking to his son. Without a word Prince Peerio turned away and went slowly off to pack his knapsack. But since his Father was banishing him penniless from the Kingdom, he had very little to put together, nothing at all in fact except a little knapsack containing one day's provisions, two clean pairs of socks, a compass, and a picture of a Princess named Lily, who lived in the Castle of Mountainy, on the other side of the world.

It was this picture which had been the cause of their quarrel. A wealthy merchant of the kingdom, who, although he was a merchant, loved good painting, had bought it a week ago for a heavy heap of gold and presented it to the Prince; and Prince Peerio, the moment he saw it, had fallen in love, not with the picture, but with the Princess. He told his Father that unless he could find Princess Lily and persuade her to marry him he should certainly live in misery for the rest of his life. But old King Stren had his own ideas of love, and especially of love at first sight, and more especially still of love at first sight of a picture. He said:

"I think not."

And he then explained to his son that it was his duty to marry Princess Killum, the daughter of a neighbouring monarch, who, besides having a large fortune, would make him a very good wife. But Prince Peerio said:

"I think not."

And then the quarrel began which ended in the King's banishing his son for ever. So Prince Peerio set out on a Sunday morning to walk round the world with a picture in his heart and knapsack. Luckily it was a very small picture and quite light. He was very sad when he thought of the quarrel, for he loved his Father and was afraid the old man would be lonely. But "It's no use worrying," he said to himself; "it can't be helped." And he determined to listen to the birds singing.

Well, he walked and he walked and he walked, and his boots wore out. So then he stopped at the town of Bremen and worked hard for a week, till he had earned enough money to buy a new pair of boots. And he walked and he walked and he walked, and his third pair of socks wore out. So then he stopped at the town of Tobolsk and worked hard for a week, till he had earned enough money to buy three new pairs of socks.

As for food, he lived all this time on roots and berries and what he could beg by the wayside. But he bought a little meat with the money that was left over when he had paid for his boots, and a little more with the money that was left over when he had paid for his socks.

And he walked and he walked and he walked, till his knapsack wore out and the picture dropped through the hole on to the ground. But luckily the ground was frozen hard at that time, so that, although the picture fell face downwards, it didn't get smudged. So then he stopped at the town of Yakutsk and worked hard for a week, till he had earned enough money to buy a new knapsack and a little more meat. And he walked and he walked and he walked, and his boots wore out *again*; so he stopped at the first large town that he came to. But it seemed as though he had been in that town before, for he found that he knew his way about the streets.

"What is the name of this town?" he asked of the first kind face that he saw.

"Yakutsk," answered the face.

"How can that be?" said the puzzled Prince; "I left Yakutsk a month ago, and I have been walking ever since."

"Let me see your map," said the face kindly.

"Alas," said the Prince, "I have no map. When I left Strenvaig, I set my course by compass and I have steered myself by that and the stars."

But at that the face looked so old-fashioned, and its owner hurried away so fast, that he didn't care to ask anybody else just then. But when he had finished his week's work, he asked his master:

"How shall I get to Mountainy Castle?"

"Mountainy," said the master, a knowledgeable fellow; "let me see — ah! — that is in warmer climes. You must turn down south. It lies south-south-east by two degrees east and then back a little way."

MAP OF THE KINGDOMS

The other underworld

KINGDOM OF STRENVAIS
Realm of King Stren

Town of
Bremen

Realm of Princess Kittum

Town of
Tobolsk

Town of
Yakutsk

The circuitous walk of prince Pasmo

KINGDOM OF
MOUNTAINY CASTLE

KINGDOM OF DRAVIDIA
Realm of prince Courtesy

So Prince Peerio bought some new socks with the money he had earned, set his compass again, and started off. But he was dispirited, because he had thought, when he set out from Strenvaig, that if he only walked by his compass, he must reach Mountainy Castle by the very shortest route. And what am I to do, he said to himself miserably, if I walk for a month and find myself back here again? But at last, after walking for two months, he learnt that he was only three miles from Mountainy Castle. It was night, and he entered a little inn: for he had saved some money from his last purchase at Yakutsk to have at the end of his journey, meaning to rig himself out a little before he went a-wooing.

"Go away!" said Mine Host, coming out of the parlour door. "I have no room at all for you. There is a big party dining here tonight, and many of them staying, and I am at my wits' end already."

Yet Prince Peerio, who had come to understand a good deal about faces in the course of his beggar's walk round the world, saw at once that the man was not really unkind but only very tired and troubled. So though he was tired out himself with his day's tramp, he said gently:

"Perhaps I can help you. I can't cook, but I am sure I could wash up rather neatly."

At once the man began to smile:

"I am sorry I spoke so tartly," he said: "It is very kind of you to offer to help. I'll tell you what. I can't give you a room to sleep in, but, demme, if you shan't have a kip in the kitchen. No sheets and blankets, you know — but at least it will be warm. I expect the Lit —

my cook — will knock you up some kind of a bed. He's a bonny little carpenter, is my cook."

Prince Peerio entered the inn, took off his coat, and started in at once to help Mine Host lay the table. Going out to the kitchen to fetch in more crockery, he noticed what an odd little fellow the cook was. To begin with, he was scarcely that high — and, besides that, he had a way of whistling and singing to himself as he went about — not regularly, but in sudden jerks and snatches; he fidgeted, too, at abrupt intervals. He would be moving smoothly and silently to and fro just like any other cook (except that he was so small), when all of a sudden he would shrug his shoulders and click out a leg or an arm in front or behind or to the side of him, his eyebrows would shoot up and his lips out, and he would whistle half a phrase of music, such as "God save our gra — " or "Speed bonny bo — " or perhaps "Mary, Mary, quite contrary, How does your gar — " and then remember himself and stop dead, and go on quietly with his work again. Prince Peerio could not help laughing at first, but he soon saw that the cook was an absent-minded little man and that the head, which seemed so very much too large for that crooked little body, was crammed full of some trouble of its own which couldn't get out.

But now the guests had arrived and were all assembled in the dining-room, talking.

" — Ha, ha, ha ..."
" — My dear sir! ..."
" — So sorry he can't come ..."
" — Ha, ha, ha, ha ..."

" — and the best of the thing was ..."
" — old Gamboy ..."
" — What? ... *No!* ... Ha, ha ..."
" — delicious soup ..."
" — Now, my dear feller ..."

That was what the Prince heard as somebody opened
and closed the dining-room door.

The Prince and the little cook were both very busy
running in and out with heavy dishes. Prince Peerio
had never done this kind of thing before. Hitherto
other people had always waited on *him*. But didn't he
enjoy it, tired as he was! What he liked most was to set
down an enormous dish in front of Mine Host, or in
front of the Vice-President at the other end of the
table, and then to whisk the covers off and watch the
cloud of steam leap up after it, like a man trying to
catch his hat. And, moreover, as he walked out into the
kitchen, he saw a tiny little porky reflection of himself
in the bright nickel-plated cover, which made him
laugh for pure joy. He had long ago forgotten how
weary he was, and when the dinner was over and the
dwarf-cook began to show him how to wash up the
dishes, he was as ready to talk as the cook was to
listen. He began at the beginning, therefore, and told
the little man all his adventures, his setting out from
Strenvaig, and his long, long tramp around the world.
At first he was greatly disconcerted by the little cook's
odd manner; for he would be explaining some exciting
adventure encountered on his journey, how once he
was robbed by a thief and another time nearly
murdered by cutthroats, when the little cook, who

appeared to be following his story with the greatest interest, would suddenly shoot up his eyebrows, click out an arm, and shrug his shoulders all in a trice, and there he would stand looking for all the world as though he had been frozen stiff in the middle of a dance. The first time the cook did this, the Prince politely stopped his narrative and waited, but "Go on, Go on!" cried the little man. "This has got nothing to do with it. I'm listening."

So Prince Peerio went on with his long story, till he reached the point where he had asked the name of the town he had been in before and was told "Yakutsk".

"How did that happen?" he paused and asked the cook. "Did I dream it? I can't have done. I remember the season changed from Autumn to Winter between my first and second visits."

"H'm," said the little man, "what map did you use?"

"No map at all. I used a compass."

"Ah, that explains it," said the cook. "You must have done just what Mercator did. *He* hadn't got a map either. In fact he went round on purpose to make one. See 'cosmic circumambulation' in the *Encyclopedia Montanica.*"

"Expound, expound," said the Prince, laughing at the little fellow's long words.

But the little fellow didn't like being laughed at.

"Very well, then," he said in a hurt voice. "Next time you have an orange, *you* try and spread the peel out flat on the table. Australia happens twice. Siberia happens twice. That's more than my advice does. Next time you ask questions, listen to the answer. Handsome is as handsome does. People who live in

glass houses shouldn't throw stones. Catch hold!" And
he threw a sopping, slippery dish to the Prince, who
deftly caught it and began drying it with a dish-clout.

For a little while they worked in silence; but when at
last they had broken the back of the job, and the great
pile of greasy clobber on the wash-board was turning
slowly into polite rows of shining plates in the rack
and dangling cups in the cupboard, and when the cook
perceived that, however quickly he washed, the Prince
could wipe a little faster and was always waiting for
him, he grew good-humoured again, and at last, as
they sat down at the yellow kitchen table to their own
meal:

"Well," he said, "what did you do it for?"

"Do what?" said the Prince.

"Why, walk round the world," said the little cook.

"Well," said the Prince, "it is true I was happy
enough at home with Stren, my Father. But one day a
wealthy merchant, who, although he is a merchant,
loves good painting, came to the palace and brought
with him this — " and he got up and walked over to
his knapsack to show the little cook his picture. But
before he could get it out, the cook held up one hand
like a policeman stopping the traffic.

"Portrait?" he said.

"Yes," answered the Prince, tugging at the frame to
get it out of the bag.

"Aha," said the little cook, archly wagging his finger.
"*La grande passion!*"

"I beg yours?" asked the Prince politely.

"*Non compos mentis*," explained the cook gently;
"it's the same thing nowadays." And laying his cheek

flat on the flat table, he looked hard at the Prince, whistled "Let the great big world keep tur — "[1] and stopped dead....

" — What pleasure it gives me to see us all here
  again tonight ..."
" — Hear, hear ..."
" — Shame! No, no! ..."
" — Tullywich, the port is with you ..."
" — this grave occasion which calls us all together, calls
  for something more than ..."

once more a burst of talking floated in from the dining-room, as somebody opened the door and went out into the yard.

"All the same," said the cook at last, lifting his head slowly from the table and addressing the Prince as though he were a baby, "let me see pretty picture!"

It was a rude thing to say, but he did not say it rudely — only as if he were very tired. For there was a clear ring of kindness in his voice, and the Prince, who had come to understand a good deal about voices in the course of his beggar's walk round the world, was not offended by it. So he took the picture over to his companion.

How startled he was by the result! For

"Princess Lily!"

---

[1] *Let the great big world keep tur* — " Of course this is not really the tune the little cook whistled, any more than the language I am writing in is the language which he and the Prince spoke. But as nobody would understand the popular songs of Mountainy, if I quoted them, it seemed better to find the English songs most like them and put them in instead. Much better.

gasped the little cook, all his queer manners fallen from him like an overall.

"What, then, do you know her?" cried the Prince.

"Yes! No! That is — I — once knew her Mother." The little man was white and trembly. "Do you love Princess Lily?" he asked.

"Love her!" said the Prince. "I — "

"Yes, yes," said the little cook, looking at him, "cut all that out, but do you *love* her?"

"Yes," said the Prince, looking at him.

"I'll help you!" said the cook, putting his hand in the Prince's.

Now the Prince looked rather old-fashioned at this, for he did not see how this little man, a cook in a wayside inn, could help him, the Prince of Strenvaig, to woo his lady. But the cook took no notice.

"The only thing I can do," he said in a thoughtful voice, "is to give you an introduction to Miss Thomson. You'll need it, let me tell you, before you've done, with a fox in the hen house like old Gamboy. Heaven knows what she may be up to nowadays."

"Who's 'Old Gamboy'?" asked the Prince.

So then the little cook, who had lived many years ago at the Castle, began to explain to Prince Peerio who Princess Gamboy was; and if it took him as long as it is taking me, it must have been very late that night before the cook knocked up a wooden bed for the Prince and they both went off to sleep.

CHAPTER XII

EARLY THE NEXT morning, with the little cook's letter to
Miss Thomson in his pocket, and a full day's wages in
his purse, Prince Peerio set out for Mountainy Castle.
When he came to the town at the foot of the hill, he
went into a shop, just as it was being opened, the
pavement swabbed, and the shutters lifted down with
a clatter, and bought himself a new lace-collar and a
new cocked hat. He would have liked to wear his suit
of bright chain-mail, but there were two reasons why
he had not brought that with him. One was that it was
rather too heavy to walk round the world in, and the
other because he wanted to approach the Castle, not as
a Prince, but in disguise. For he wished to find out all
about the people in the Castle before he told them why
he had come. He thought himself very lucky, therefore,
when, on arriving at the Castle gate, he saw a stable-
boy leaning idly against it.

This stable-boy was a good-natured hobbledehoy
young lout, all legs and wings, who yanked about the
Castle in a suit of corduroy reach-me-downs, with a
straw hanging out of one side of his mouth and a
melancholy whistle tootling out of the other.

"Mornin'," he said to the Prince.

"Good morning to you!" answered Peerio pleasantly.
Very soon they fell talking, and Prince Peerio began to
ask the stable-boy what was going on inside the

Castle. The little cook at the inn had already told him what had gone on while *he* was still at the Castle, but he didn't seem to know much about what had happened since. He had not been at the Castle since Princess Lily was born, so he said, and that was nearly twenty years ago.

"Yes," said the stable-boy gloomily, "things is going from bad to worse inside. Old Gamboy, she's got 'em all into the coop, like a lot o' chicks, an' she's sitting on the lid — and there she'll stay, I reckon, as long as she's on top of dirt."

He shook his head sadly from side to side, and the straw hanging from his mouth wagged to and fro as solemnly as the pendulum of a grandfather's clock. Then, out of the other side of his mouth, he went on talking:

"Them *Amalgamated Princesses!*" he said indignantly. And, after a pause: "Anyone 'ud think the Castle belonged to 'em. 'Is por old Majesty stuck in his study from morning to night, not knowin' what's goin' on and not darin' to come out and see for hisself. They do say as if he so much as shows 'is face at the door, old Gamboy is up and fussin' all over 'um, before you can say 'Sneeze.' '*Well*, dear, *wot* is it, me dear? Troublin' that por old 'ead of yours, *are* you? Better leave it all to me, *darling*, much better leave it all to me. Yes, Lily's quite well, me dear, *I'm* looking after 'er.' O Lord, 'aven't I 'eard all about it from the parlermaids? Aven't I 'eard it more than one times?"

Prince Peerio's heart leaped when he heard the stable-boy say "Lily," but he said nothing, for he wanted the lad to go on.

"They do say," he continued at last in a hoarse whisper, leaning forward to the Prince's ear, "as he just sits an' stares! sits in 'is study all day, just starin' an' starin' at nothing. 'E don't seem to know quite where 'e is, por gentleman. P'raps it's a good thing 'e don't. I tell you, when I 'eard ten years ago that 'e was married to 'er — yer could have knocked me down with a feather — just like that, yer could! — knocked me down with a feather! Nobody knows how it 'appened. I don't believe 'Is Majesty knows 'imself. They say 'e just kinder woke up one morning an' found it *'ad 'appened* — started callin' 'er 'is Queen. I don't wonder neither, seein' as she'd been bossing 'im about enough for fifty Queens ever since 'er sister died. But the queer thing is, Mister, they say as 'e don't always seem to know be rights who she is. 'E mixes up the old an' the new in 'is por old 'ead — calls 'er Violet, yer know."

By this time the Prince and the stable-boy, without knowing what they were doing, had entered the Castle grounds. The stable-boy went on:

"I tell you I don't like it at all. You should have 'eard 'er talkin' down in the market-place, when the famine was on. I wasn't but a little nipper then; but, my, she said some nasty things. My Father believed 'em all, too — marched up to the castle, 'e did, the night the Queen died."

But Prince Peerio had heard all this from the little cook at the inn. So he interrupted:

"What are the *Amalgamated Princesses*?" he asked.

"Ah!" said the stable-boy.

"Well, what are they?"

"*She* knows!" said the stable-boy, darkly squinting.

"Doesn't anybody else know?"

"Not properly they don't. But I'll tell you, Mister: I know one thing, and that's not two!" He leaned forward and whispered again. "They pays 'er subscripshuns. An' she *spends* 'em — spends 'em all on 'erself and 'er own fenarious schemes!"

"Embezzles them," suggested the Prince.

"That's it, Mister, the first thing she did with 'er bloomin' subscripshuns, as didn't properly belong to 'er, was to purchase that great black book of hern. An' she spent the rest of 'em *hex*perimenting with the magics in the book. I tell yer, it fair gives yer the creeps to walk underneath her window at night an' hear the old lady up there a mumblin' and a mutterin' to 'erself or the Devil, it's pretty much the same thing, I reckon. An' them *Amalgamated Princesses*, they still goes on payin' their subscripshuns, oh yus, they still go on payin' up through the nose. They seem ter like it. There's nought so queer as folk, I reckon — very!"

They were talking so hard that they never noticed they had come right up to the Castle wall and were standing underneath Gamboy's window.

But Aunt Gamboy, up in her room, bending her head low over the squiggled pages of *Excerpta*, had heard their footsteps. She perked up her head, and her dark eyes gleamed suddenly with a baleful light. She crept to the window. She could see them. She could hear every word they said.

She heard Prince Peerio ask the stable-boy where Princess Lily was and what she was doing.

The boy pointed to a building a little way outside the Castle grounds; it was a high, stalk-like tower, with a little door at the bottom of it and at the very top a few narrow slits of windows. The rest was blank, staring stone.

"She's in there," he said.

And then Gamboy heard him tell the Prince what follows:

When the Princess Lily had at last recovered from her long illness, she was so wasted by fever and so weakened by pain that her own Father could scarcely recognize her. Nor was she indeed the same girl. Ever since the day Aunt Gamboy had had tea with her she had been peak-faced, irritable, and headachy. A silence had fallen on her. She would never open her mouth of her own accord, and, if she was asked a question, would answer "Yes" or "No," and say no more. If anybody asked her to do anything, to play at ball or go a walk, she would only look peevish and avoid complying. She no longer read the wise and beautiful books on her Father's shelves, nor did she dance any more, as she had danced to him in the old days for joy, but sat about in drooping attitudes with her white hands hanging listlessly in her lap, thinking.

She was a burden to all who came near her, and all were astonished at the change. Her own servants, who had delighted to serve the gay young thing she once was, now avoided her whenever possible, and pouted back sour and sullen looks at her querulous upbraidings. But there was one thing which nobody noticed (nobody, that is, except old Lord Tullywich, and he saw most things that went on under his nose), and that was that Princess Lily had grown timid. She, who had never trembled until she saw the toad, was now ready to be scared by her own shadow, terrified by the darkness, and startled out of her skin by the banging of a door two rooms away.

Often, just before she went to bed, she would run to Gamboy and cling on to her hand:

"Auntie," she would say, "will you promise me that no toads will get into my room tonight? They won't, will they?" And Aunt Gamboy would turn her head and look down at Lily through her great round spectacles, and say, oh so kindly:

"I can't *promise*, my darling — it's very unlikely — it's never happened before — and I sincerely hope it never will; but — they *may* of course. Anything *may* happen, you know. You mustn't be frightened, there's a good girl."

Then Princess Lily would answer obediently (for she was still obedient to her Aunt):

"No, Auntie. I only thought I'd just like to ask you."

And then she would go off to bed, trembling with fear, and lie awake half the night with her eyes wide open, staring into the darkness. All the time, as the days went by, she came more and more to lean on her Aunt, to go to her for comfort, and to believe every word she said. So that if Gamboy had once told her firmly (what was no more than the truth) that no toad could possibly get into her room as long as she kept the windows shut, she would have slept quite happily every night; and very soon she would have been peak-faced and white no more, but as healthy as it is possible for anyone to be who sleeps with the windows shut.

But Aunt Gamboy never told her this.

As for her Father, she scarcely ever saw him now. For he, too, had come to lean all his strength on his new Queen. He believed himself to be happy, because he no longer thought much about anything — not even about Violet. But he was not really happy.

So Queen Gamboy gradually gathered all the affairs of State into her own hands, and at last even began to attend the meetings of the Privy Council in her husband's place, while he sat mooning in his study. As a matter of fact, she used to put slumber-syrups in his coffee. Ever since their marriage she had insisted on making it for him with her own hands, and ever since their marriage the King had grown sleepier and sleepier. So that poor, pale little Lily scarcely ever saw her Father nowadays, or, if she did see him, he seemed only half to know her, and would make some foolish remark or other about the weather or the political situation. *He* could never tell her that she was safe from toads. He didn't even know she was frightened of them.

So at last, at the Queen's suggestion, she had had the high, stalk-like tower built for her. But even there she did not feel safe from toads.

And there she sat all day and every day, with her hands in her lap, staring. Books all round her, and she never read one of them; pictures, and she never looked at them. She did not know the history of her own country, and she might have learnt the history of the world. Indeed, so far from knowing its history, she did not even know how it was made or what it was made of. Every spring the wild flowers burst into a sea of

blossom that foamed up against the very foot of her tower, Honeysuckle, Loosestrife, Ladysmock, Daffodils, Goldilocks, Orchises, Palm, and the Drooping Star of Bethlehem — and she never troubled to learn their names. The birds perched on her high little window-sill, and said "Jug-jug" and "Deedle-deedle", but she could not tell one from the other; and at night the constellations, Orion and the Great Bear, looked in, but she did not know them apart. She did not even know the difference between a star and a planet. What is the good of knowledge? she said, and began to forget all that her father had taught her. Nothing seemed to her to be worth doing, for nothing she did brought her any pleasure. Nor could she think of anything for long at a time except toads. At night she dreamed of them.

In his own words the stable-boy explained all this to Prince Peerio. He did not know all I have told you. What he did know he had only heard from the Castle servants. But he knew enough to make the Prince understand. For months, nay, for years now, the Castle, he said, had been like a painted castle. There was a spell on it. The King silent in his study all day and the Princess shut up in her tower. Even the servants went about their work with hushed voices and glum faces. A silence like death seemed to have come upon them all. One person only seemed alive. One person moved to and fro with a purpose — Queen Gamboy. She, too, was silent, but not with the silence of death. She was silent rather as ants and spiders are silent, and it was with their swift hurryings that she glided to and fro.

Now when the stable-boy had finished his story, he nodded to the Prince and loitered away to the stables. But the Prince stood still, pondering deeply how he might win Princess Lily to be his Queen. For nothing that the stable-boy had said had changed his love for her. He only longed more than ever to marry her and to give back to her her joy in life.

Somebody else stood still, too. Up in her window, a little way above his head, Queen Gamboy was standing still, thinking. And as she thought, she frowned. She had overheard every word of the talk between the Prince and the stable-boy. What is more, she had heard the trembly sound in Peerio's voice, when he asked after the Princess Lily.

She was no fool, wasn't Queen Gamboy.

"Aha!" said she to herself. "A poor chance for your schemes, Gamboy, my dear, if this young fellow is to come and set us all by the ears, because he happens to have seen a picture of my niece. And just when we're all getting on *so* comfortably, too! I couldn't stir up those fool citizens down there in the town to rebel, even when they were starving. So it's plain they must have *some* king or other over them; but if there's to be another king in Mountainy after King Courtesy, it shall be my son — mine — Queen Gamboy's." And she scowled fiercely at the looking-glass — partly because she hadn't even got a son yet.

"That young man wants taking down a peg or two, I fancy!" she muttered, and she peeped out of the window to see if he was still there. Yes, there he was, standing underneath the window, dreaming like a loon. Gamboy tiptoed across her room to the table and picked up *Excerpta*. Softly, with the great black volume under her arm, softly she crept back across the carpet to the window.

He was still there.

Now she opened the book at a page she knew well enough and began (softly) to murmur her spell. She whispered it, whispered it lest he should hear and start away, before it had time to work. And as she whispered it, she moved her corky arms to and fro, engraving wicked rhombs and pentacles on the empty air.

Now I cannot tell you the exact words she uttered. If I did, the same thing might happen to you that happened to Prince Peerio. Not exactly the same thing, of course, unless the story is being read aloud to you and the person who is reading it happened by chance to make the exact patterns in the air which Gamboy made. But even if all this should not be so, even if you are reading the book to yourself, quite enough might happen to make you very, very uncomfortable. Aunt Gamboy had been studying that book for years now, you see, and her magic had grown very much stronger since the last time she used it, which was when she made her own and Princess Lily's teeth chatter up in the Royal Nursery, ten years ago. These, then, were something like the words she whispered (but not the exact words):

"No dimber, dambler, angler, dancer,
Prig of cackler, prig of prancer,
No swigman, swaddler, clapper-dudgeon,
Cadge-gloak, curtal, or curmudgeon,

No whip-jack, palliard, patrico;
No jarkman, be he high or low,
No dummerar or rapparee,
Hobson, jobson, jigamaree,
Nepot, niminidoxy, duffer,
Nor any other will I suffer
To prevent me from transmogrifying that young man."

No sooner had she finished than the dreaming Prince came to himself with a jerk. He felt sick, wondered where he was, and in the twinkling of an eye saw his stomach shooting out in front of him, and felt his eyes bulging from his head. And now Gamboy craned her scraggy neck over the window-sill and gave a long sorcery chuckle to see on the ground beneath her, just on the spot where Prince Peerio had been standing a moment before, a great grey-green lolloping toad!

CHAPTER XIII

POOR PRINCE! As he felt the icy change come over him, he cried out and clutched by instinct at his most valuable possession, the picture of Princess Lily in his knapsack. But the cry simply turned into a dismal reedy croak, and instead of the picture his little legs closed on something else. And since he clutched hold of it with a part of him that had already been changed, it stayed in his grasp. If he had caught it a moment sooner and with his own human hands, it would have vanished with them, when they vanished. If he had reached for it a moment later, it would already have been swallowed up like everything else, his knapsack, his boots, and his buttons and all, in the change. But luckily for him he got hold of it at exactly the right moment, and when he recovered himself enough to look about him, he perceived that he was holding between those little legs the letter of introduction to Miss Thomson, which had been given to him by the little cook at the inn. He would have wept (if toads could weep) because it was the letter and not the picture which he had retained. He did not know that that was really the most fortunate thing that could have happened.

At first he squatted there on the ground in despair, not knowing what had happened to him, and hopeless of ever regaining his human shape. He nearly broke down; but he was a brave toad, and not to be dismayed by anything that befell, however dreadful. So he set about thinking. Then he guessed that Queen Gamboy had something to do with the matter. What was he to do?

He took up the letter in his mouth and began trundling off to find Miss Thomson's cottage in Tyttenhanger Lane.

But he took such a long time to get there, partly because toads can only move very slowly and partly because he could not ask anybody the way, that we shall have to go back and see what happened at the Castle while he was on his way.

That stable-boy was a very lazy fellow. When he had finished talking to the Prince and had got back to the stables, "Oh dear," he said to himself, "I suppose there is nothing to do now but work": and he saw the long morning stretching out ahead of him with nothing but grooming, grooming, gloomy grooming till he had groomed the whole double row of horses that stood there with their heads to the wall and their tails hanging down behind. He picked up a curry-comb and began slowly cleaning a brush: "S—s—s—s—s," he said, to make it sound as though he were working dreadfully hard; then he dropped the curry-comb, yawned, and as he yawned happened to look up into the stable roof.

There he saw the trap-door that led up to the loft above the stables.

"I'll go get some more hay down," he said, meaning to have a quiet nap up there among the sweet-smelling hay. So he fetched a ladder and climbed up through the trap-door into the hay-loft, and he was just going

to throw himself down on a pile of hay, when he saw
something gleaming in the far corner of the dark loft.
It was half covered by a stack of dirty, used-up straw,
and he couldn't think what it was, so he yanked with
his great hob-nailed boots across the loft and pulled at
the bright thing, till it came clear of the straw that
covered it. He had never seen anything like it before.
First he turned it over and over in his hand. Then he
wiped it clean on his red pocket-handkercher with
white spots, saying as he did so, "S-s-s-s-s" through
his teeth, just as though he were grooming a horse.
And then, at last, when he had wiped the mouthpiece,
he put it to his mouth and blew through it.

Rooty $^{\text{tootity}\,\text{tootity}\,\text{tootity}\,\text{tootity}\,^{\text{too.}}\,\text{Too}\,\text{tootity}\,\text{tootity}\,\text{tootity}}$ too.

And with the very first sound of the trumpet,
another sound, a sound that had been going on in the
stables all this time, suddenly ceased. This was the
noise of horses. For they had stopped chumping hay
and stamping and shambling with their feet, and all of
them were standing stock stone still in rows, like
marble horses. And their tails hung down behind
them straighter than ever. And at the very first note
of the trumpet (for it was heard in the Castle too), all
the porters and doorkeepers and sweepers and cooks
and bakers and pastry-makers in Mountainy Castle
stopped carrying and doorkeeping and sweeping and
cooking and baking and pastry-making, and looked at
each other and listened. And at the very first sound of
the trumpet King Courtesy, lolling in his study half-

asleep, half-awake, dreaming of nothing on a sofa, started bolt upright, and cried out with a loud voice:

"Violet! Violet!"

And at the very first sound of the trumpet Aunt Gamboy drew in her scraggy neck from the window, and sat down upon her bed, and began to be so unhappy, so unhappy, dreaming of the time when she was a little girl called Gambetta with a sister called Violetta. But Princess Lily, alone up there in her tower, also heard the Silver Trumpet. And she had never heard it before. And she wondered. She wondered why she was mewed up there, when other Princesses walked about the world beneath the open sky, and she wondered what would happen to her as she grew old, and if she would spend all the rest of her life in that one little room in the tower, and what the world was like.

Rooty $^{\text{too.}}$ Rooty $^{\text{too.}}$ Rooty $^{\text{too-oo-oo.}}$

As the last note died slowly away, everybody in the Castle stirred slowly, like a man waking from sleep, and looked mazedly round him. Many of them opened their mouths to ask what had happened, but, just as they were about to speak, they seemed to change their minds, they looked away, they dropped their eyes to the ground as though they were ashamed of something, as though they all knew something which they were all pretending they didn't know. And as the last note died slowly away, Princess Lily looked up and said: "What was that noise?" and she sounded a little bell for her maid-in-waiting to come, and when she came, scolded her for allowing vagrant musicians to play within earshot of the tower; for it was against all orders. Then she began to dab her forehead with cold water and ordered a dish of tea. And as the last note died slowly away Aunt Gamboy frowned and said:

"Tut!"

and, getting up from her bed, craned out of a window to catch a last glimpse of the toad, that had once been poor Prince Peerio, lolloping awkwardly away over the lawn to the Castle gates. And as the last note died slowly away, the light left King Courtesy's face, and he sank back on the sofa with only a vague troubled look in his eyes.

But as the last note died slowly away, the stable-boy was so pleased with the sound the trumpet made that he put it to his lips and blew again. Once more the sound floated out from the stable, across, and in at the windows of the Castle. Once more Princess Lily began to wonder, and then suddenly she knew that she was very unhappy.

"I must help myself!" she cried, and before the sound had died away, had rung her little bell once more and told the maid-in-waiting who came to answer it:

"Send a messenger at once to Miss Thomson, Bee Cottage, Tyttenhanger Lane, and ask her to come and see me."

Once more Aunt Gamboy sat a-dreaming, and then, if you had been there, you would have seen a queer change come over her face; the corners of her mouth began to turn up, the wrinkles to leave her forehead, and her eyes to lose their look of cunning. It seemed for a moment as though she were turning into another person. But then, as the sound ceased, her face slipped back, and she became all Gamboy again. And some say that, this time, Violet herself, deep down in her grave, heard the Silver Trumpet, and that she stirred and trembled there, and that her face too began to change, taking new wrinkles to its white brow, and that a look of cunning began to creep into her eyes underneath their coverlet of darkness.

But when King Courtesy heard the trumpet for the second time, he started up, ran to the door of his study, and called out in a voice that was itself like a trumpet:

"Who is doing that, who is doing that? Send him to me!"

For the trumpet reminded him too keenly of his beloved, and made him sadder than he could bear. So they found the stable-boy and brought him to the King, and the King threatened to execute the stable-boy, but forgave him when he heard that he had found the trumpet by accident and did not know who it belonged to. And then Courtesy took the Silver Trumpet from him, and locked it up in a cupboard in his study, and pronounced the death penalty on any man who should put it to his lips again. After he had done that, he sank back again upon the couch and buried his face in his hands.

But the stable-boy went down the hill into the town, and told the citizens all that had happened. Now the citizens were getting very tired of Gamboy's arrogance, for she was a hard Queen. And when they heard the stable-boy's story of the Silver Trumpet and of its strange effect upon their King, they smelt a rat, they did. "She has deceived *us*," they said, remembering the time of the famine. "Why should she not be cheating the King and our poor Princess? Why are they both so wretched?"

Therefore they determined to march up to the Castle once more and to demand an audience of their King. And it would be ill, they said, for Queen Gamboy, if they found aught amiss.

This they determined to do on the following day but one, for the next day was a Sunday.

CHAPTER XIV

MEANWHILE, PRINCESS LILY'S messenger had started off on horseback to find Miss Thomson, and it was not long before he reached Bee Cottage, Tyttenhanger Lane. He gave Miss Thomson his mistress's message, and asked her if she had any answer he might take back with him.

"Yes," said Miss Thomson, "tell your mistress that Miss T. always helps those who have the courage to ask her. I will come."

So the messenger went posting back with his answer, and a hundred yards from the Castle gate narrowly escaped crushing with his horse's hoofs a toad which was lolloping wearily along the road in the other direction. For that was as far as poor Prince Peerio had managed to get in all this time. You see, he found it so difficult to get along with the letter in his mouth, because it stopped him from taking breath easily.

As soon as the messenger had left her, Miss Thomson put on her sugar-loaf hat and her little old cloak, took her stick, and started out on foot for the Castle. It was not very far, and soon she perceived coming towards her a great grey-green toad. How surprised she was, when she saw that it had a letter in its mouth, and how much more surprised when she stooped down and saw that the letter was addressed to herself! At first the toad would not let go, but she spoke to it and said that she was Miss Thomson. Then the toad let go. It let go of the letter and waited while she read it. And when she had read what the little cook at the inn had written in the letter, Miss Thomson bent her peaky nose right down to the toad's ear and began whispering in it.

"I am sorry," she said, "that *I* cannot turn you back again into a prince. There is only one way of doing that, and that is if somebody loves you and cherishes you *as you are now*, in the shape of a toad."

Alas! thought Peerio to himself, who will do that to a hideous, icy creature like me? Must I spend the rest of my life like this?

But Miss Thomson read his thought and answered it. She spoke to him for a quarter of an hour, telling him exactly what he must do. And he listened and laid well to his heart all her counsel. Then, as she went on her way, he lolloped off the road into a ditch and rested there; for there was no longer any need for him to go to her cottage.

When Miss Thomson arrived at the tower, Princess Lily had almost forgotten why she had sent for her, for the sound of the Silver Trumpet was no longer in her ears. Therefore she had grown languid again, and she began talking to Miss Thomson as though she were one of the Royal Physicians, complaining of headaches and sleeplessness, and moaning peevishly of the wretchedness of her lot. But all Miss Thomson said was:

"What do you want?"

"Oh, I'm so miserable — such a wretched, useless creature."

"Well then, what are you afraid of?"

"How do you know I am afraid of anything?"

"You must be afraid of something, if you are a miserable, wretched, useless creature. What are you afraid of?"

"Nothing. That is — I am afraid of — I don't like — that is, I hate the idea of — of — " (she would not mention the word).

"Of what?" said Miss Thomson sharply.

"Of t — of toads," answered Princess Lily, and began crying softly.

Miss Thomson's voice grew kinder.

"And why," she said, "why, pray, should you hate one of God's creatures more than another? Eh?"

Princess Lily had no answer. And now she remembered what her Father had said to her all those years ago on their way home from their walk, in the afternoon, before she had told Gamboy about the toad. "Only weak and silly people scream, when they see mice and spiders and toads," he had said. "You must get to know them and you mustn't be frightened."

"I don't know," she answered humbly. "I'll try not to."

"That's right," said Miss Thomson. "You must get to know them. And shutting yourself up in this tower all day is hardly the best way about it, is it?"

"No — no," said Lily, through her tears.

"I suppose you think that being afraid of a thing is a reason for running away from it?"

"W-well," said Lily doubtfully. "It does seem to be rather a good reason."

At that Miss Thomson paused and looked thoughtful. Then she smiled good-humouredly. Then she grew serious again and said slowly:

"Ye-es, but as a matter of fact it isn't. I can't tell you why: you'll have to take that from me."

And then she said:

"Do you want to be like the Princesses in the books your Father used to read to you?"

Princess Lily did not answer; for after Miss Thomson said that, far away, deep down, deep down in her memory she heard her Father's voice reading aloud to her the stories of Alcestis and of brave Imogen. She thought of all those happy evenings, when she was a little girl, when he had read to her, and when she had danced to him in the light of the hanging lamp. But then she thought of her Father, as he was now, growing old alone in his study, and of herself, shut up alone in her dismal tower. How long was it since she had heard his voice or even since she had danced a step? All this she thought of, but she did not answer Miss Thomson.

"Silence gives consent," said that lady at last.

Then she leaned forward and, talking for a quarter of an hour in a low earnest voice, told Princess Lily what she must do if she wished to make herself once more into a real Princess. After that, Miss Thomson departed, and as on her way home she passed the ditch where that toad was resting itself, she called out to him:

"Tonight!"

and passed on without waiting for an answer.

That night, for the first time in eight years, Princess Lily slept alone. For she had resolved to do everything that Miss Thomson had told her to do. She was frightened of being alone after dark; therefore, as soon as it grew dark, she called all her maids-in-waiting round her, and all the men-servants whose duty it was to guard the tower, and told them to go away and sleep in the Castle. She was dreadfully frightened of sleeping in a dark room, and every night for eight years had had a little night-light kept burning in her chamber, so that she could see the walls. Therefore tonight, before she went to bed, she put out that night-light. And oh, she was dreadfully, dreadfully frightened of opening her little window, for the creepers grew up to it from the ground, and she feared — she dared not say to herself what she feared. Therefore tonight she opened that little window as wide as it would go, and lay in her bed looking at the star that peeped in through it.

Sleep? She couldn't even stop herself trembling. The darkness seemed like a black stuffy bag which someone had dropped noiselessly over her head. Over and over again she moved as though to get up and light the light, and if there had been anyone below in the tower, she would have called out for companionship. But then she would say to herself, "Hold on tight, Lily, hold on tight, and be a Princess," and with that she would clench her fingers hard upon her thumbs, or grasp a handful of the bedclothes and cling tight to them to keep the Fear away.

And when the Fear grew almost too great to bear, and the creepers rustled in the wind, and the moaning wind flapped the curtains against the walls of the dark chamber, and the floorboards creaked as though someone were tiptoeing upstairs to her, she would give one great lonely sob and say to herself:

"They can't do worse than kill me."

And then:

"I can only die once."

And again:

"Death is better for me than another eight years like the last."

Nevertheless her heart stood still, as she heard something drop down from the window-sill on to the floor of her room. For she knew, without seeing it, that it was a toad.

But when, in the darkness, Prince Peerio heard the loud thumping of her heart, a great pity for her smote him, so that he yearned to cry aloud and to speak comfortably to her. But he could not, for he could not speak at all.

Yet, amid all her terror, Princess Lily knew what she must do. And when she had kissed the toad upon its icy head, and cherished it, the moon, which had risen in the meantime behind a bank of clouds, stood forth suddenly and shone into the little room. And there was no longer any loathsome toad on her bed, but there in the middle of the chamber, his chain-mail flashing silver in the moonlight, stood a beautiful young Prince. And when she arose from her bed, he took her in his arms. Nor did Princess Lily ever know Fear again, either in the darkness or in the daytime.

CHAPTER XV

IT WAS NOT very long before the Prince went away into the adjoining room to wait while Princess Lily dressed herself. "I wonder," he thought to himself, "how I come to be wearing this suit of chain-mail which I thought was at the other side of the world."

He did not know that it was not his own chain-mail at all, but a brand-new suit, which old Miss Thomson herself had fashioned for him out of dreams, and put upon him, while the toad was walking, and he himself was only a dream. But it was.

Then he returned to the Princess, and all night long they sat together talking, until the moon sank down in the west, and the sun arose and looked in at the casement. And although she had never seen him before, Princess Lily knew that Prince Peerio was her Prince. She told him all about her life at the Castle, of the horrible dreams, and how unhappy she had been all those long years and years. But, as she told him of it, the unhappiness seemed to vanish even from her memory, so that now it all seemed unreal, her life in the tower, her sickly headaches, and her fears.

And then, because that great weight had been pressing on her heart for so long and was now lifted from it suddenly, as suddenly she wept. So that if there were left in her any dregs of sorrow at all, the sweet tears washed them away.

When she was herself once more, her first thought
was for her Father, and she told Prince Peerio that if
he could win King Courtesy back to be his old self
again, he would indeed have made her the happiest
Princess in the world.

Very carefully had the Prince listened to all she told
him of affairs at the Castle, and especially, at the end,
to her account of hearing the Trumpet-call. As he
listened, he remembered also sundry things which the
little cook at the inn had told him; for he too had
spoken of a Silver Trumpet.

Now he was a very wise young Prince (wise in his
schooldays, and wise when he started out from home).
And not for nothing either had he walked all alone
round the world, and been turned into a toad at the
end of it. Such adventures are very uncomfortable
while they last, but they give a man understanding.

So he knew what to do.

First of all he packed off a messenger to the inn to
fetch the little cook, for he could not forget how much
he owed to his letter of introduction. That was the first
thing he did.

Then he set out to find Aunt Gamboy.

Aunt Gamboy was up in her privy chamber,
addressing a large mass-meeting of the *Amalgamated
Princesses*. I shan't tell you what she was saying to
them, for it was very much like what she had said
before to the citizens of Mountainy from her tub in the
market-place. Very much like it. And, moreover, she
was telling them all to go back to their own countries,
in disguise, and there, upon tubs in the different
market-places, to say what she had said, and to

arouse rebellion and discontent among the citizens. For there was distress at that time in many of those countries. Gamboy was promising, if they would do this, to make them all Queens of those countries.

And they believed her!

But she had no intention at all of doing any such thing. Oh no. For now that she was Queen, she no longer wished her own subjects to be discontented, but she very much wanted the citizens of all the neighbouring countries to rebel. For then, thought she, when they are all in confusion, I will make old Courtesy send great armies among them, and I will subject them all to my rule, and my son shall be King of half the world, Amen.

Then Prince Peerio walked in.

Well, he went straight up to where Aunt Gamboy was standing speaking, he took hold of her, and he bounced her up and down on the floor, just as though he were driving piles, or hammering a nail into his shoe with a poker, or knocking in stumps with a cricket-bat. He did that until he had fairly shaken the breath out of her. Then he did that again. Then he took her under his arm like a bolster and marched plonk out of the room with her.

And when he had gone for two or three minutes, those astonished *Amalgamated Princesses* shut their mouths again; but not before.

He walked straight into the office of the Head Gaoler. He put Queen Gamboy down on the table, and he said to the Head Gaoler:

"Here!"

Then he went out of the office and up to King Courtesy's private study, knocked at the door, and went in.

The King was drinking coffee and staring at the cat. The Prince said:

"Good morning, sire. Your daughter is being married tomorrow morning at ten."

But the King only stared at him in a silly way.

So he went to the cupboard, took out the Silver Trumpet, and came downstairs with it. Then he called the Castle servants about him, and bade them make all preparations for a magnificent wedding. Then he returned to Princess Lily.

"But, dear," said she, when he told her what he had done, "how am I to marry you tomorrow when I have no wedding dress?" With that he sounded a little bell, and in came the first maid-in-waiting, who stood there and listened while he told her what to do.

At last the next morning came, and with it the time for their wedding. There was Princess Lily in the beautiful, wide, white dress which her mother, the Queen Violet, had worn on her own wedding-day (for such were the orders Peerio had given to the maid-in-waiting). And there was Prince Peerio himself in his shining suit of bright silver mail with a silver casque on his head and a nodding grey plume to it.

Just before the wedding four stately bearers were sent with a royal litter to the King's chamber to carry him down. And at first, when he came, he saw nobody, and peering with his white face from the curtained litter seemed not to know where he was. But when he saw Princess Lily standing in her mother's dress — "My daughter!" he said, and stepped down from the

litter. At the same time, by the Prince's orders, Queen Gamboy was released from gaol and given leave to attend the wedding. Nor did she stand humbly at the back among the onlookers, as might have been expected, but came boldly forward and stood with sullen, scowling face beside her niece.

Some of the Castle servants, eager to please their new master, started forward to hale her away from there; but Lily stopped them with a wave of her hand and bid them let her be.

Now when the wedding was over and they came out of the Church into the sunlight, Prince Peerio stepped forward, and taking the Silver Trumpet from his baldric, placed it to his lips.

And the sound that came from the mouth of the Trumpet was:

Rooty tootity tootity tootity tootity too. Too tootity tootity tootity too.

Rooty too. Rooty too. Rooty too-oo-oo.

Whereupon the procession stood very still, listening, and waiting for the noise to die away. But just as silence fell, and all were about to move forward again, the Prince raised the Trumpet to his lips a second time, and blew:

Rooty tootity tootity tootity tootity too. Too tootity tootity tootity too.

Rooty too. Rooty too. Rooty too-oo-oo.

Then a third time, and a fourth he blew, and again and again and again, till the air rang to the sweet silver din, and all the world seemed rocking about them like a steeple. Then it was that all eyes were turned upon the Queen, and men saw what they would hardly believe afterwards that they had beheld. For again the queer change came over her face, again the corners of her mouth began to turn up, the wrinkles to leave her forehead, and her eyes to lose their look of cunning.

And still the Trumpet rang on, till the air about their ears felt as solid as water and shook as tempestuously. Her features went on changing and sliding into one another, like clouds over the sky, moving and clearing until there, beside her husband, white-robed and laughing in the sunlight, stood none other than Queen Violet herself!

"Where is the Silver Trumpet?" she cried at once, as she awoke, and looking anxiously round her: "where is the Silver Trumpet?"

"Here, Your Majesty," said Prince Peerio, walking up and handing it to her with a low reverence.

She took it and gave it to King Courtesy.

"Guard it," she said; "guard it in the future even at the cost of your life."

Whereat the stooping King straightened his old back as by a miracle. Now the vague meandering look went out of his clear eyes, and taking the Silver Trumpet from Violet's hands, he kissed her: "Most gracious lady," he said, "most gracious lady," and broke down and wept, declaring that they would guard it together. And so they must have done, for it was never again lost from Mountainy Castle.

And some say that deep down in the grave other features upon another face had been changing too and sliding — that to this day a body, which is Aunt Gamboy's, lies buried in that churchyard. But no man can point to her grave, and therefore many do not believe in it. For the tombstone that had V. R. engraved upon it, now that Violet was alive, was gradually let fall into ruin, and soon men began to say that there never had been a grave in that spot. And in less than thirty years they were saying that there never had been anybody called Aunt Gamboy at all. But others pointed to the things she had done, to the *Amalgamated Princesses*, for instance. Why else should they be Amalgamated? And they would also point to the high, stalk-like tower, crumbling now and disused, where Princess Lily had spent so many years of her life. Why should she have hidden herself away up there, they would ask, if Aunt Gamboy had not fastened her claws into her heart? And again, why, they would say, should old King Courtesy have all those white hairs, and Queen Violet none, if Aunt Gamboy had not led him such a dance above the earth, while Violet was sleeping quietly beneath it? So the two parties would argue with one another, and never agree. And as time went on, it became harder and harder to decide which party was right. And it will go on getting harder still, I expect, unless this very story should travel as far as Mountainy. For then of course everybody will know that there certainly was an Aunt Gamboy — very much so. Everybody, that is, except those who will swear it is a forgery. But that is really looking too far ahead.

Now as soon as Prince Peerio saw that King Courtesy and Queen Violet had finished embracing one another, he went up to King Courtesy, who stood bareheaded in the sunlight, trembling with amazement and joy, and handed him his sword. And he asked pardon courteously for the way in which he had taken upon himself to order the King's servants about that day and the last, hoping that the King would forgive him.

"You shall order them about as you please," said the King, "for from this day forth you are King of Mountainy, and Lily my daughter is Queen."

Whereat there was a great shout, and again the Silver Trumpet rang through the air, while the old King and his new-found wife took both hands, threw their hands back, and danced round each other, singing:

> "And Lily my daughter is Queen,
>   Tra-la-la.
> And Lily my daughter is Queen."

Up the hill came the citizens — tramp, tramp, tramp — singing in a low threatening tone:

> "Here we are, here we are,
> To make Queen Gamboy sing *sol-fa*."

But when they reached the church and heard the news, they cast away their pitchforks and axes, and flung their caps in the air, crying:

"Long live King Peerio and Queen Lily!"

and spread themselves over the grass plot outside the churchyard.

Then from the other direction a party of seven were seen approaching with rapid steps. It was old Miss Thomson, bringing with her the five musicians in the pink coats and curly grey wigs, and yellow stockings, for she had foreseen (witchery old lady that she was) that there would be rejoicing that day, and she had sent for them where they dwelt. But the seventh person was the little cook from the inn.

King Peerio recognized him as he drew near, and sprang forward to greet him and shake his hand for gratitude. But before he could reach him, somebody else sprang forward too, in front of him, crying out:

"Little Fat Podger! Little Fat Podger!"

It was Courtesy. And now, old white-haired Lord Tullywich came forward, and kneeling before his King explained in a thin quavering voice how he had disobeyed his orders, telling him that the Little Fat Podger had died in gaol, whereas in truth he had recovered from his illness; but he, Lord Tullywich, had not had the heart to put him to death. So he had sent him away into hiding at an inn some three miles away, where he and his friends sometimes met for dinner and fun.

"Your Majesty will remember," went on Lord Tullywich humbly, "that I told you the Dwarf had passed quietly away, and so indeed he did; for he passed quietly away to the little inn under my protection!"

Of course the old King forgave him at once, and thanked him royally for knowing, like a good servant, when to disobey orders.

But the Little Fat Podger himself had not spoken yet, and everyone waited in silence now to hear what he would say. He could only look round smiling and nodding at everyone, with tears in this eyes, saying nothing at all. Yet some of those who stood nearest to him, thought they heard him murmuring to himself:

"All those years washing dishes — it's as wholesome as a shoulder of mutton to a sick horse — to a sick horse, you know."

And then suddenly one leg shot out, and he would have begun to dance, only he was getting too old now, so he drew it in again thoughtfully, and was heard murmuring to himself:

"*And the side-step step — and the side-step step — and the side-step, side-step, side-step* — anything jocund!"

You can imagine what rejoicings there were then — what reunions! Between Courtesy and Lily, between Violet and the Little Fat Podger, between Violet and the citizens, between Violet and Lily, who had only been two days old when she last saw her. You can imagine what shouting and laughter there was in the sunshine that morning upon the green plat of grass. Nor was it very long before the fiddlers struck up, and King Peerio himself called the first tune. And these dances were quiet enough for the Little Fat Podger to join in — yes — and even old Lord Tullywich cut a caper or two, for all his white hairs. On and on and on they danced, citizens and courtiers, lords and ladies, kings and queens, till the sun had gone down in the west, and the sky over their heads was cool green and gold. And then they all gathered in a knot round the fiddlers and danced a very old country-dance called "Mr. Barney's Breeches". And that was the end.

PUBLISHED WORKS BY OWEN BARFIELD

First published

Books by Owen Barfield

The Silver Trumpet	1925
History in English Words	1926
Poetic Diction: A Study in Meaning	1928
Romanticism Comes of Age	1944
This Ever Diverse Pair	1950
Saving the Appearances: A Study in Idolatry	1957
Worlds Apart: A Dialogue of the 1960's	1963
Unancestral Voice	1965
Speaker's Meaning	1967
What Coleridge Thought	1971
The Rediscovery of Meaning, and Other Essays	1977
History, Guilt and Habit	1979
Orpheus: A Poetic Drama	1983
Owen Barfield on C. S. Lewis	1989
Night Operation	2008
Eager Spring	2008
The Rose on the Ash-Heap	2009
The Tower: Major Poems and Plays	2021
The Riddle of the Sphinx: Essays	2023

Translations and edited works of Rudolf Steiner

World Economy: The Formation of a Science of World-Economics (trans. with T. Gordon-Jones)	1936
Anthroposophy: An Introduction	1961
The Case for Anthroposophy	1970
Guidance in Esoteric Training (trans. with Charles Davy)	1972
The Year Participated: being Rudolf Steiner's *Calendar of the Soul* translated and paraphrased for an English ear	1985

Edited works by other authors

Man and Animal: Their Essential Differences, by Hermann Poppelbaum	1960
The Voice of Cecil Harwood	1979